Pick Your Path!

RollerCoaster TYCOON

Pick Your Path!

Spaced Out!

By Bobbi J. G. Weiss and David Cody Weiss
Cover illustration by Neil Stewart

Grosset & Dunlap • New York

. . . .

"Happy birthday, Chanine!"

Chanine Williams grinned at her three friends. Today was her birthday, all right, and she was about to enjoy her best present ever—a free day at the brand-new Kosmos Space Park!

She gazed at the enormous flying saucer that served as the park entrance. It looked as if it had crashed into the hillside, so its ramp was crooked and its open hatchway tilted a little. *Is it real?* Chanine wondered. *Did friendly Space Brothers really land on Earth in this spaceship?* Her heart almost skipped a beat at the thought of the rumors about Kosmos being true. *Maybe there really are aliens here! Oh I hope I hope I hope it's true!*

Veena Tranh, her best friend, snapped her fingers. "Earth to Chanine! Hey, this is your day, girl. Let's get moving. I may have gotten us the tickets, but you're in charge, remember?"

"Oh man, do you have to put it that way?" moaned Rob Rossi, a short boy with a video camera in one hand, an electronic data pad in the other, and a cell phone clipped to his belt. "Now she'll boss us around all day."

"Nah, she'd never do that," said Kev Bryon, and he flexed the muscles of his right arm. "Space Babe knows who's the boss around here."

Chanine rolled her eyes and grinned. "I'm here to meet aliens, Kev."

"There's the magic word," Rob sighed. "*Aliens.* Chanine, how can you possibly believe there are real aliens here?"

"Haven't you heard the rumors?" Veena asked him. "Everybody's talking about it."

"Yeah," said Kev. "There was that article in the school newspaper just last week, and I've even heard them talk about it on the local news."

"I heard it on the Space Brothers website," said Chanine. Chanine liked to surf the net, and more than anything she loved the Space Brothers website. It was the one place where she felt truly comfortable chatting with the hundreds of other people who believed in aliens just like she did.

Rob snorted in amusement. "Come on, you guys. The rumors about real aliens here are just that— rumors. It's a marketing tactic to get people to buy tickets."

"Which we did, so let's go!" urged Veena.

Chanine led her friends up the flying-saucer ramp. Her eyes bugged wide when they reached the ticket counter—a blue-skinned fish-faced woman with scales and webbed fingers took her ticket and placed a sticker on her hand. "This is your day pass," the woman said in an odd, bubbly voice. "Do not lose it."

Chanine was sure the woman was a real alien, but she didn't have a chance to ask what planet she was from—the eager crowd pushed her forward, through the turnstile and into the flying saucer. "Wait!" she said, trying to go back, but then she saw the inside of the saucer and forgot all about the fish woman.

A three-headed alien in a flowing robe loomed over her, projected on a forty-foot-tall video screen. "Welcome to the Kosmos Alien Embassy," the giant creature boomed. "I am Galactic Ambassador Oobja."

"Oobja, huh?" said Rob, sounding skeptical as usual. "Let's see—if he's got three mouths but only two hands, how does he brush his teeth at night?"

"Rob," said Veena, "do you always have to be a smart aleck?"

Rob pretended to think hard about that. Then he said, "Yes!"

Chanine was barely listening. She was too busy staring up at the four video screens next to Oobja's screen. The images of four other aliens were projected there, each from a different planet. Under each of their screens was a doorway that led to a different Zone in the park. "Come on," she said. "Let's hear about the Zones before we decide where to go first."

Following the other people in line, Chanine led her friends to the first Zone entrance. "I am Sothoth of planet Cryptikon," said the alien on the giant video screen. It was a frightening mass of slimy tentacles and fangs. The arched doorway leading to the Zone that represented its home planet was covered with wriggling snakelike...*things.* "Visit Cryptikon and be terrified," Sothoth hissed.

The next Zone entrance was a metal tunnel. "I am Mep Gnog of Transitor," said the alien on the screen above it. Mep Gnog was part flesh, part machine, and its voice sounded mechanical. "Visit Transitor and marvel at our wondrous technology!"

The third Zone entrance was small—so small that adults had to stoop to walk in. "I be Spun't'ii of Minuta," said the alien on the screen above it. He was only the size of a dog, and his voice was high and squeaky. Chanine grinned at the weird way he used verbs. "Be welcome to my world, humans, but be warned—we be small, but we be mighty!"

The fourth Zone entrance was formed by an incredible arched aquarium filled with fish and plants. The alien on the screen above it looked just like the fish woman at the ticket booth, but this was a handsome male. "I am Bluudohba of Aquaria," he said in a bubbly voice. "Step forward and visit our wondrous water world!"

"Aquaria," Chanine murmured. "So that's where she's from."

"Who?" asked Veena.

"The fish chick at the entrance," said Rob. "Chanine, it was just a costume."

"Oh, Rob, quit being a dork," Veena told him.

Rob opened his mouth to reply, but he was

interrupted by a voice over the loudspeaker. "Will the Chanine Williams party please come to the Visitor's Desk?"

Chanine looked at her friends in alarm. "Did we do something wrong?"

"Nope," said Veena. "C'mon." As if she knew what it was all about, Veena led them to the Visitor's Desk at the far end of the Alien Embassy saucer. "We're the Chanine Williams party," she said to the man behind the counter. He wasn't wearing any kind of alien costume, just a suit.

"Welcome," said the man. "Please give to me your Day Pass stickers."

"But...what's wrong?" Chanine asked, peeling her sticker off.

"Nothing is wrong," said the man. "Miss Veena Tranh has arranged for our special Kosmos Birthday Package." He held out four golden stickers. "These are Gold Day stickers. They'll allow you to go to the front of all lines, for rides or food or souvenirs. You won't have to wait."

"Cool!" said Rob, pressing his sticker onto the back of his hand. "Veena, good job!"

"I know," said Veena smugly. "Now you owe me one, dork."

Chanine gave Veena a hug. "Veena, you're the best!"

Veena smiled at her best friend. "So, Chanine,

where should we go first?"

Chanine thought a moment. "Let's ride Parallax."

The boys groaned. Parallax was a slow gondola ride that went from one end of the park to the other at 200 feet in the air. "That's perfect," said Veena. "That way we can get an overview of the whole park first. C'mon, everybody!"

Parallax wasn't particularly exciting, but even Kev had to admit that seeing the layout of Kosmos Space Park was impressive. But something else was even more impressive—the park staff. Almost all of them looked like aliens. Even Rob was impressed by the costumes.

Chanine, of course, was convinced that she was seeing real aliens. "See? That guy has four legs!" she said, pointing. "No way is that a costume!"

"It's special effects stuff from Hollywood, Chanine," said Rob, but he took video using his zoom lens anyway.

By the time the ride was over, Chanine was so excited she could hardly speak. "Did you see them all?" she kept saying. "Oh my gosh, there really are aliens here!"

Veena laughed. "Then which ones do you want to meet first?" she asked, winking slyly to Kev and Rob.

Chanine calmed down and considered the four

Zones. "I'd rather not start with Cryptikon or Minuta," she decided.

"But we have to go to Cryptikon!" said Kev. "That's where Nemesis is!"

Chanine knew that the main reason Kev had come to Kosmos was to ride Nemesis, "the world's scariest ride." He wanted to be an astronaut, so he worked out each day, loved doing extreme sports, and challenged himself at every opportunity. He'd probably ride Nemesis nonstop all day if he could.

"I've interviewed a lot of people on the Space Brothers website," Chanine told him. "I've come to the conclusion that our Space Brothers aren't scary and they aren't little, so the real aliens here in the park can't be Cryptikonians or Minutans."

Rob snickered. "Chanine, that website is filled with a bunch of goofballs—nothing personal."

"It's okay, Rob. I forgive you," said Chanine. She knew that Rob didn't believe in the Space Brothers one bit. In fact, he'd come to Kosmos to get evidence to disprove the rumors of real aliens. He intended to put that evidence on his website and become famous.

Rob liked to disprove "urban myths," such as the famous story of the hitchhiking ghost or the girl with the 1960s "beehive" hairdo that became filled with real bees because she never washed her hair. He was fascinated by how people often believed impossible stories—or what *seemed* to be impossible stories. Chanine, on the other hand, liked to think she had an open mind.

Veena put an arm around Chanine's shoulders. "The birthday girl has spoken, boys. We're either starting at Aquaria or Transitor. I vote for Aquaria."

"No, no, Cryptikon," Kev insisted. "C'mon, Veena, I'm dying to ride Nemesis. How about this? Rob can come with me to Cryptikon while you go with Chanine to Aquaria. You and Rob have cell phones. We can meet up again later."

"That's fine with me," Rob said. "As long as I get my evidence, I'll be happy."

"I'd prefer that we all stay together," said Chanine.

Veena sighed. "Well, let's not stand around talking about it all day!"

It's your decision! Should the group split up or stay together? And where should they go first? Pick your path!

- **If the group splits and you want to follow Chanine and Veena to Aquaria, go to page 9.**

- **If the group splits and you want to follow Rob and Kev to Cryptikon, go to page 13.**

- **If the group decides to go to Transitor together, go to page 17.**

Chanine looked at Kev's eager expression. "Oh, okay," she told him, grinning. "Go ride Nemesis with Rob. We'll meet up later."

Kev gave a hoot and ran for the stairs, followed by Rob.

Veena smiled at her friend. "On to Aquaria?" she asked.

"On to Aquaria!" Chanine confirmed.

When they reached the Aquaria Zone, the girls navigated their way along a network of bridges, crossing over the vast alien "ocean" known as the Paxis Sea to reach the entrance to the Imploder ride. Imploder was a roller coaster with airtight capsules so that riders could be taken underwater to the Aquaria Mall.

The girls showed their Gold Day stickers to the ride operator and were seated in the very next capsule. Just for fun, they started screaming before the ride even began. When they got going, they screamed for real. Imploder hauled them straight up into the air, looped them around three times, then zoomed them straight back down again. They hit the water with a splash and rocketed through the cool blue Paxis Sea.

Their capsule finally slowed down and entered a rock tunnel that served as an air lock. Once their capsule was inside, the tunnel door closed behind them and all the water was drained. Then a door ahead of them opened to reveal a normal air environment beyond—the underground Aquaria Mall. Their capsule exited the tunnel, gliding on a set of tracks, and stopped at a debarking platform. Their door popped open.

"That was awesome!" Veena wheezed, stumbling out.

Chanine followed, giggling. "Help!" she said breathlessly. "I can't stop laughing!"

The girls finally recovered and scouted out the territory. Aquaria Mall was filled with shops and restaurants, a stage for live performances, and an arcade. Veena wanted to check out the stores, which sold both human and "alien" merchandise, but Chanine wanted to "make contact" right away.

Much to Veena's embarrassment, Chanine tried to talk to every "alien" she saw. Worse, she kept trying to speak to them using so-called "alien" phrases she'd gotten off the Space Brothers website from people who claimed to have been abducted. Veena knew most of the phrases well by now, especially "Klaatu barada nikto"—whatever that was supposed to mean. Usually Veena had no patience for Chanine's weird alien hunts, but today was her birthday, so Veena let her do what made her happy. She even agreed to take some photos of Chanine standing with "real Aquarians!"

There was one truly strange occurrence in Aquaria. The girls were greeted by name every time they passed through a door. "WELCOME, CHANINE AND VEENA," a mechanical voice would say, or "THANK YOU FOR SHOPPING WITH US, MISS WILLIAMS AND MISS TRANH." Things got even stranger when an Aquarian saleslady greeted them by name. Chanine thought it was great, but Veena started getting the creeps.

"How do they know our names?" she whispered to Chanine, while they checked out a rack of colorful fishy-scaled blouses.

"Aquarians must be telepathic," Chanine answered, as if it were obvious.

"That doesn't explain the machines."

Chanine put her hands on her hips. "Clearly, they have technology far beyond ours. Their machines must be telepathic, too."

"No way!" Veena said. "It's got to be some new ID technology to make us think the aliens are real." She looked at her Gold Day sticker. "I bet it's the stickers! I bet they contain little circuits or something, and our names were encoded in them when I bought the Kosmos Birthday Package!" She sighed with relief. "Yeah, that's it. I knew there had to be a logical explanation." Then she spotted the Aquaria Arcade. "Ooo, I challenge you to a game of SPLATTER!"

Chanine grinned. SPLATTER was a video game that simulated paintball. "You're on!" she said.

They raced to the arcade. "I scored high five times

• • • • 11

in a row last week," Veena reminded Chanine. "You're gonna lose."

"Ha!" was all Chanine said, as she slipped a token into the SPLATTER machine.

The game began.

Who's going to win the SPLATTER game? It's your choice!

- **If Chanine wins, go to page 21.**
- **If Veena wins, go to page 23.**

"Well, there's only one thing to do in a situation like this," said Rob. He reached into his pocket and took out a quarter. "Heads, we stay together. Tails, we split."

The others agreed, and Rob flipped the coin. It came up tails.

"Yeehaw!" Kev said happily. "I promise we won't take long, Chanine." He hurried down the stairs that would take him from the Parallax platform down to ground level. "Come on, Rob!" he said, snaking through the crowd and taking the steps two at a time. "Nemesis, here we come!"

"Hey!" said Rob, trying to keep up. "I'm a couch potato, dude! Slow down!"

Even though Parallax had left them on the far side of the park, all they had to do was hop on the Orbit ride to get to any Zone. Orbit was a quick tram that circled the park, stopping every minute to let off passengers and take on new ones. In no time at all, the boys stood on the main concourse of Cryptikon.

The Cryptikon Zone was creepy. The walls dripped. The ground was sticky. The air was strangely humid, and dark shadows loomed everywhere. Snack booths featured things like Slime Shakes and Gobble-Goo candy. Rob laughed as he videotaped a tray of french fries that wriggled. He wanted to check out some of the grotesque creatures that were selling souvenirs, but Kev said, "Just one ride on Nemesis, and then you can tape whatever you want, okay?"

So they dodged through the crowd and made it to the front of the Nemesis line. The human ride operator saw their Gold Day stickers and nodded. "Here," he said, and he gave them each a device that looked like a wristwatch.

Kev read the label. "Fright-O-Meter? What's it going to do, tell us how scared we get?"

The ride operator nodded. "Don't think it's easy to stay in the green. Almost everybody tops the red line."

Kev and Rob got into a four-person car along with a young couple, and the ride slowly started to climb. "I'm scared, John," said the girl to her boyfriend.

"Ah, don't worry, ma'am," Kev told her. "We'll be swinging free once we gain enough height, and then we'll just corkscrew a couple times, drop straight down at 90 miles an hour, and then go through a black tunnel upside down. No sweat."

Rob chuckled as the girl went white and then— well, all he did was scream after that. Nemesis threw them in all directions, and Rob felt like he was in a giant spin-dryer. Before he knew it, the ride was over.

"Yyyyyyes!" roared Kev, leaping out of their car. "Let's do it again!"

Rob barely managed to climb out of the car. "Hey, look," he mumbled, his knees wobbling. "My Fright-O-Meter is so beyond the red zone...I think it broke."

"Look at mine," said Kev. "I stayed in the green the whole time!"

Both boys jumped as a loud bell suddenly rang. Lights flashed. A spooky voice over a loudspeaker hissed, "Someone has set a new park record, ladies and gentlemen!"

A creepy alien that looked like a cross between a giant stork and a pile of mud oozed up to Kev. Rob turned on his video camera, as the creature held out a gooey hand to Kev. "You are just the kind of human we are looking for," it said. "How would you like to test yourself against something much more difficult?"

"A ride better than Nemesis?" said Kev. "You bet!"

"Hey, alien guy," said Rob, aiming his camera at the creature. "I bet your real name is something like Harold, right? How long does it take you to get into that fancy costume every morning, Harold?"

The creature smiled. "Not long," it hissed, and turned back to Kev. "Now, my young friend, follow me for an even greater challenge."

Kev took Rob's arm. "Come on, Rob. We can't pass this up."

• • • • • • • • •

"Maybe you can't, but I can," said Rob. "You go ahead with Harold. I'd rather snoop around a little. Let's meet back here in fifteen minutes."

Kevin and Rob know what they want to do now. Do you?

- **If you want to follow Kev and the alien to the mystery challenge, go to page 25.**

- **If you want to follow Rob on his hunt for anti-alien evidence, go to page 27.**

"The birthday girl wins again," said Veena. "We go together to Transitor!"

The four friends hurried down the stairs that took them from the Parallax platform down to ground level. Then they boarded Orbit, a speedy tram ride, to quickly reach Transitor. Once there, they stepped off the tram into what looked like a town square, except almost everything was made of metal, including the ground, the shops, and even the trees. And everything seemed to be mechanical, from the talking signs to the walking trash cans. The aliens themselves seemed to be either full robots or half-robot-half-man creatures like Mep Gnog.

"Man, this is great!" Rob said as he videotaped the scene. "You can't tell where the people end and the hardware begins!"

"I think that's the point, genius," said Veena.

"Greetings, Chanine Williams," said a squatty little robot. "Please accept a map of the Transitor Zone."

Chanine took the map it offered, her eyes wide, and watched the robot scuttle away. "Did you see that? It knew my name!"

"It probably read your Gold Day sticker," said Rob, tapping the sticker on the back of his hand. "I've been reading about new ID technologies. I bet these stickers have a chip inside that tells the machines who we are. It's probably one of the ways they're

• • • • • • • • •

trying to make people believe the aliens are real."

"Or it might be real alien technology!" Chanine said excitedly. "Somebody on the Space Brothers website said that there's a machine race on Alpha Centauri that—"

"Oh, no," Rob said. "No goofball website stories, please."

"But maybe Transitor is their name for what we call Alpha Centauri," Chanine went on, undaunted. She ran over to a boxy alien sitting on a bench. "Hi! Can I ask you a question?"

The alien—or whoever was inside the costume— couldn't smile. It had a metal face. But it managed to nod its square head. "Of course, Chanine Williams."

Chanine looked back at her friends. "See? This one knows my name, too!"

Rob and Kev shook their heads, as Chanine had a short conversation with the boxy alien. "I tell ya, that girl is too weird," said Rob.

"And you're not?" said Veena, grinning.

Chanine ran back to them. "Her name is Kampk, and she's not from Alpha Centauri. She said Transitor is a whole different planet way far away."

Rob nodded. "Of course it is. Did you happen to see a zipper in her costume?"

Chanine blinked. "What?"

"Never mind."

"Let's ride Black Hole," said Kev. "It's in

this Zone. I heard it simulates a trip through a subspace wormhole."

"I've heard of wormholes!" said Chanine. "I want to see one! Come on!"

They hurried to the front of the Black Hole line. "Greetings, Chanine Williams and guests," said the robot ride operator.

"This is so exciting!" said Chanine happily. "They *all* know us!"

They took their seats in a car on a steel tube track. The ride started slow as it climbed upward, then they thundered straight down and everything became a blur. The speeding car curlycued, rotated 180 degrees, and then headed toward an awesome wormhole effect. Everybody held up their arms and screamed as the coaster hurtled them toward what looked like a black wall with nothing but a pinprick opening at the center. Then, suddenly, they were through it and coasting to a gentle stop.

"That was easy," Kev said, hopping out of the car as if nothing had happened.

Chanine and Veena slowly climbed out, giggling and leaning on each other, leaving Rob to wobble out on his own. "Easy, my shorts," he said. "I think I left some major organs back there."

"I want a soda!" said Chanine, and she dashed off to a concession stand. The others followed.

As a golden Transitor Service Robot with four

• • • • • • • • •

arms served their drinks, it asked, "Did you enjoy the Black Hole ride, Chanine Williams?"

"Whoa," said Kev. "They can even keep track of what we do here?"

"I told you, it's all marketing," Rob said. "By the time we're done, they'll—" He stopped when the Transitor Service Robot jerked strangely. One hand fell off, and smoke came out of its nose.

"Ex-Ex-Excuse m-m-me!" it stuttered. "Mal-Mal-Malfunction! Require re-re-re-pair-pair!" It rolled away and disappeared around the back of the concession stand.

Veena stood up. "Let's follow it."

"We're not supposed to go back there," said Chanine.

Rob stood up, too. "I'm with Veena. If I can get a shot of somebody repairing the robot costume, I'll have my evidence that no real aliens exist here."

"I just want to see what it does," said Veena, her eyes bright with curiosity.

Veena and Rob are awful curious about that malfunctioning robot. What about you? Do you think the group should follow the robot or not?

- **If they decide to follow the robot, go to page 32.**

- **If they decide not to follow the robot, go to page 30.**

20 • • • •

The SPLATTER machine buzzed, and Chanine's control panel lit up. "I win!" she said triumphantly.

The arcade attendant, a young Aquarian male, stepped forward. "Congratulations, Chanine Williams," he said in a gurgly voice. "We of Aquaria would like to give you a gift, both for this victory and to honor this day of your birth. Would you come with me, please?" He gestured toward a door near the back of the arcade.

Chanine grinned. "Oh, this is so cool! Let's go!"

"Chanine," Veena whispered. "You can't just wander off with some stranger!"

"He's not a stranger," Chanine answered reasonably. "He's an Aquarian."

"But—" Veena began, only to be cut off as Chanine took her arm and pulled her along.

The alien led them through the unmarked door and down a long ocean-blue corridor. "It is not far," he told them. "Just around this corner."

"Okay," Veena whispered to Chanine after a moment, "I guess I am a little curious. I mean, first they know our names, and now…" She trailed off when Chanine stopped walking. "What is it?"

Chanine was staring at a door with a strange symbol on it. The symbol looked sort of like a fish, sort of like a dragon, and it was twisted in a circle. "That looks familiar," she said thoughtfully, studying it.

· · · · · · · · · ·

"You probably saw it on a Kosmos ad," said Veena. "Come on."

"No, really," said Chanine. "I know this symbol. It means...something. Something important." She looked at her friend. "I have to go inside, Veena."

"Now you're just being weird," Veena argued. "Don't you want your free gift?"

Which way should the girls go?

- **If they continue to follow the alien, go to page 34.**

- **If Chanine opens the door with the strange symbol on it, go to page 36.**

After a furious battle, the SPLATTER game console beeped. "Told you!" Veena crowed, doing a little victory dance. "I am the SPLATTER Queen!"

Chanine calmly replied, "Maybe I let you win. Maybe you've been so nice to me on my birthday, I decided to give a present back."

"Oh right," Veena laughed. "Nice try." She noticed that her friend was looking at something. "What is it?"

Chanine just started walking, heading for an Aquarian woman with her small son. "You've been watching us," Chanine said to them. "How come?"

Veena tried to pull her friend away. "Uh, Chanine, what are you doing?" she whispered. "They're just employees in—"

"I like this one, Mommy," gurgled the "alien" boy, pointing at Chanine. "She's funny."

Chanine stooped down to look more closely at him. "Am I?" she asked with a smile. "Then tell me what this means—*Klaatu barada nikto.*"

Veena rolled her eyes and was about to poke Chanine in the arm when the Aquarian woman gasped. Veena turned to see four big, muscular Aquarian men in armor coming toward them. The nearby crowds hooted and clapped, believing that the display was just another Kosmos spectacle.

• • • • • • • •

The Aquarian woman turned to Chanine. "I'll protect you!" she said.

Is this threat real? Should Chanine and Veena trust the alien woman? You decide!

- If the girls accept the Aquarian mother's protection, go to page 41.

- If the girls take their chances with the Aquarian guards, go to page 44.

Harold the alien—Kev couldn't help but think of him as Harold now—led the way through an unmarked door, down a narrow staircase, and into a room that contained a round travel pod the size of a small car. The pod sat inside a long clear tube that ran all the way across the room and through the far wall. Kev couldn't see where it went beyond that.

"You have operated what humans call *video games*, have you not?" Harold asked. When Kev nodded, Harold opened the pod to reveal a complex control panel full of flashing lights and dials. "This is a space flight...simulator. It is soon to be available to the public as a new attraction, but we are inviting especially talented players to perform a test run."

Kev stared at all the controls. "I'd love to play, man, but no way do I know how to operate all this. It's not like any video game I've ever seen."

"I will teach you the...rules," said Harold. He held up a small wandlike device and tapped it against Kev's forehead.

Kev felt a rush of heat in his head. When he looked at the control panel again, he understood it—every button, every dial, and every switch. "Whoa," he said. "Instant knowledge! How'd you do that?"

"A new learning technology," Harold said, and stepped aside so that Kev could climb into the pilot's seat. "Your mission is simple. You are to pilot this pod into orbit and dock with Space Station Zeta. I

• • • • • • • • •

wish you luck." Harold closed the pod door.

Kev looked around the interior of the capsule. *This is so neat!* he thought. The new knowledge in his head told him how to buckle into the seat and how to do a systems check. Then he flicked a yellow switch to make a viewscreen appear on his right. It displayed a map of Earth, the moon, and the surrounding space. *This will be a snap!* he thought confidently. Next step, start the engines.

He pushed a button, and the pod shuddered. *Oops! Wrong button. I can't put out the docking gear until I get to the space station!* He punched another button, retracted the docking gear, and then correctly started up the engines. The roar was loud, and he could feel the vibrations through the pod. "Harold, my man, this is some simulation," he muttered. "Everything looks and feels so *real!*"

Holding the joystick gently but firmly, Kev piloted the pod through the travel tube. The pod gained speed, and as the tube banked upward, Kev revved up to launch speed. The pod roared out of the tube and into the sky.

"Yahoooo!" Kev howled. "It's like I'm really flying!" He steered the pod up into outer space....

Will Kevin win the game? You decide!

- **If Kev flies like an ace, go to page 46.**
- **If Kev doesn't fly so well, go to page 50.**

26 • • • •

Rob watched Kev leave with Harold the ugly alien. *Now that's what I call a great costume,* he thought. *Too bad I couldn't spot a single seam or zipper in it.* He looked around. *What I need is to find an employee who's just going off-shift, or somebody whose costume is too hot. One shot of them taking off their head and pow!—so much for the Kosmos alien rumors.*

Holding his video camera at the ready, Rob started down the Cryptikon concourse. He looked everywhere—around concession stands, in the shops, even behind the bushes. But he didn't see anything unusul except some really disgusting details of the so-called planet Cryptikon, such as a fountain of black grease and green roses that smelled like dirty socks. He tried to interview some of the "alien" employees, but they were too busy doing their jobs to talk that long.

Finally, he spotted a droopy monster-guy heading down a side path. *He looks pretty tired,* Rob thought. *I bet he's just finishing his shift.*

He followed the droopy monster down the path, which wound behind some bushes and ended up at an Employees Only door. *Bingo!* Rob thought, watching the monster shuffle inside. He waited a moment, caught the door just before it clicked shut, and slipped inside.

The corridor beyond was completely white and

• • • • • • • •

there were no doors, at least none that Rob could see. He held back until the droopy monster had shuffled around a corner. Then he tiptoed after it.

One turn, two turns, down another long corridor, another turn—Rob kept following the monster, wondering where it was going. He passed several doors with labels like POWER and MAINTENANCE and CONFERENCE ROOM, but nothing that indicated a costume storage room.

Finally the droopy monster stepped into a room. Rob waited a few seconds, then followed. *Bingo!* he thought. It was a locker room, and the droopy monster was standing next to an open locker. Rob lifted his video camera and, leaning out from around the corner, pressed RECORD. *Take your head off!* he hoped. *Take your head off!*

That's exactly what the droopy monster did.

Rob's eyes bugged wide. Underneath the alien monster head was *another* alien monster head—a *worse* alien monster head—a REAL alien monster head! It was bald, and instead of a face it had a mass of wriggling tentacles. *There's no way that's a costume!* Rob thought, too scared to stop taping. *I'm looking at a real alien from Cryptikon!*

Holding back a moan of terror, Rob continued taping as the Cryptikon alien set its costume head down. It took off its gloves to reveal fingers like snakes. It took off its boots to reveal feet with dozens of thin, wriggling toes. Rob just gawked through his camera viewfinder. *I've got to get out of here!* he thought wildly.

Something snatched his camera out of his hand. "What—?" Rob began, but he got no further. Slimy hands grabbed him by the shoulders. Hot stinky breath blew in his face. Three pairs of bright red eyes glared down at him.

He was surrounded by aliens.

Can Rob possibly escape? It's up to you!

- **If Rob is dragged away by the aliens, go to page 53.**

- **If Rob wriggles free and runs for it, go to page 56.**

• • • • • • • •

"We'd better not," said Chanine. "Honest, Veena. I don't want to get in trouble."

"But what about my evidence?" said Rob.

Kev spread his arms wide. "We have this park for the whole day, Rob. I'm sure you'll find something."

"I think I've found something already," said Veena, and she pointed. A robot was rolling down a path on wheeled feet. "That can't be a human being in a costume," Veena continued. "It must be over seven-feet-tall, and it's way too skinny."

"Look how it balances on those wheels," said Kev. "No way do we have robot technology like that."

Rob held up his video camera. "I say it's some kind of trick. Let's check it out."

This time Chanine agreed, since the robot was on a normal visitor's path. So the four friends hurried after it, weaving through the crowd, trying not to let the robot know it was being followed. When it ducked through a door that said MAINTENANCE, they had to stop.

"Rats!" said Rob.

"Let's follow it anyway," said Veena.

Kev was willing, but Chanine hesitated. "I told you guys, I don't want to get thrown out of the park," she said.

The problem solved itself when the MAINTENANCE

door opened again. Out rolled four small robots that looked exactly like the big one. "It split into four pieces!" Chanine murmured in wonder.

"Oh right," said Rob sarcastically. "Chanine, there's no such thing as—"

"They're getting away," Veena whispered. "Argue later."

So they resumed the chase. The four little robots stayed in a group and led them all the way to the Minuta Zone entrance. "Of course," Chanine whispered. "They're small. Everything in Minuta is small. They must actually belong *here*, not in Transitor."

They entered the Minuta Zone just in time to see the four little robots split up—two rolled right and two rolled left. "We've got to split up, too," said Rob. "Chanine and I will go right. You two," and he pointed to Veena and Kev, "go left. Keep in touch by cell phone."

The others agreed, and they split up.

Rob, Chanine, Kev, and Veena know which direction they want to go. Which direction do you want to go?

- **To follow Rob and Chanine, go to page 60.**

- **To follow Veena and Kev, go to page 63.**

· · · · · · · · · ·

Veena led the way to the concession stand. "Just stand casually until nobody's looking," she whispered to the others. When the coast was clear, the four of them darted behind the stand.

They were just in time to see the golden Transitor Service Robot go through a door marked SERVICE ENTRANCE. Veena hurried to the door and caught it before it clicked shut. Everyone slipped inside.

There was a long white hallway on the other side. The golden robot was rolling along, its arms still flailing. Smoke still came out of its nose, and it bumped into the wall a few times before disappearing around a corner.

"Come on," Veena whispered.

They tiptoed down another hallway, around another corner, and then stopped when the robot entered a room. They inched up to the door, which was labeled REPAIR. From inside, they could hear strange sounds—clicks and bumps and mechanical whirring. Veena gripped the door handle and ever so slowly eased the door open a crack.

Everybody crowded behind her to peer into the room. It was big inside, and filled with several Repair Robots. They didn't look as nice as the golden Transitor Service Robot. The Repair Robots were nothing but tall boxes with glowing eyes and a dozen jointed arms, each arm holding a different repair tool. They had already opened up the malfunctioning

Transitor Service Robot and were in the midst of repairs.

Rob started videotaping the scene, but he'd hardly pressed RECORD before all the Repair Robots turned to face the human intruders. "WHO. ARE. YOU?" they demanded together.

It looks like Veena, Rob, Chanine, and Kev aren't as sneaky as they think they are. What should they do now? It's up to you!

- **If they decide to answer the Repair Robots' question, go to page 67.**

- **If the four friends are too scared and run away, go to page 65.**

· · · · · · · · ·

Chanine hesitated, gazing at the symbol on the door. "I guess you're right," she finally said. "I probably saw it on an ad. It's just so neat looking, I thought it...I don't know...meant something."

"Yeah, it probably means this is the Aquarian Zone dressing room. Now let's go before somebody walks out in their underwear," Veena joked.

Chanine resumed walking. The arcade attendant led them around the corner and to another door. "After you," he said, standing aside. Chanine opened the door.

"SURPRISE!" shouted a crowd of people inside.

Chanine took a step back in shock. "A-a party?" she stammered.

"Yup!" said Veena. She led her friend inside, where they found both their parents, friends, lots of "Aquarians," and even Rob and Kev. "But you guys went to Cryptikon!" Chanine said when she saw the boys.

"We were supposed to make you think that," said Rob. "I think we deserve an Oscar, don't you, Kev?"

Kev gave Chanine a wink. "It's called a red herring, Space Babe. Fooled you!"

"Happy Birthday, sweetie," said Chanine's mother, kissing her daughter on the cheek.

Her father gave her a big bear hug. "You're so crazy about aliens, we decided to throw your party here at Kosmos."

• • • • • • • • •

"And in honor of the occasion, I have brought my highest representatives," said a familiar voice.

Chanine turned to see Bluudohba, the Aquarian who had greeted them in the Alien Embassy. He was flanked by several other dignified Aquarians. Veena leaned over and whispered in her ear, "Honest, they're just people in costumes, so don't go bananas."

Chanine giggled as Bluudohba gave her an "Honorary Alien" certificate and—she grinned—a beautiful silver necklace with the symbol that had been on the door. Apparently it was the Aquarian "national emblem."

Chanine hugged her parents and her friends. "Thank you, guys," she told them. "This is the best birthday I've ever had!"

THE END

Chanine couldn't help it. Something beckoned her to the door, so she opened it and stepped inside.

Veena turned back to the arcade attendant and found him smiling. "You should go in, too," he told her.

Veena didn't understand. "You wanted us to go in there all along?"

"I hoped you would. Come." He led her inside.

The sight that met Veena's eyes was too bizarre to believe. She stepped into a huge room filled mostly by a tank, like a giant fish tank, only there were no fish inside. There were Aquarians in the tank—*real* ones who could breathe underwater!

While the Aquarians at the Mall had small fins and small webs between their fingers, the ones in the tank had large fins on their backs, arms, and legs. The webbing on their fingers and toes was extensive, making their hands and feet look like paddles. The gills on their necks opened and closed with each breath they took.

Chanine was staring at them in wonder. Veena joined her as one of the fish people in the tank waved. "Hi, Chanine! I'm your cousin Mrrryn!"

"Excuse me?" Veena asked.

"All will be explained," came a familiar voice. Veena and Chanine turned to see Bluudohba, the Aquarian who had greeted them via video when they'd first entered Kosmos.

Chanine grinned at him in delight. "You're real," she said. "All of you. I knew it! I knew there were real aliens on Earth!"

"Oh, there's much more to that story, young one," said Bluudohba in his gurgling voice. "Let me show you something." As Veena watched, he guided Chanine to a device that looked like a lamp. He positioned her under it. "This simulates the spectrum of the Aquarian sun," he explained.

"What are you doing?" Veena demanded.

The arcade attendant put his hand on Veena's shoulder. "Don't be afraid," he told her. "Watch."

Bluudohba hit a button. The lamp cast a bright yellow light down on Chanine—and she began to *change*. A fin poked out from her back. Smaller fins poked out from her legs and arms. Finally, a fin grew up out of the top of her head like an elegant crest. She held up her hands—her fingers were webbed. She touched her neck—she had gills now as well as lungs.

Veena almost fainted.

Chanine, on the other hand, grinned wider than ever. "I'm an alien!" she gurgled.

"You are Princess Prya," Bluudohba told her. "You were brought to Earth as a child so that you might grow up here, in a human home. That way, when the time came, you would be able to help bring Aquarians and humans together."

A door at the back of the room opened, and four people entered: a man in a U.S. Army general's uniform, a woman in a U.S. Marines uniform—and Rob and Kev!

"Space Babe," Kev said softly, as he gawked at Chanine.

"Man, you are so right," Rob murmured in awe.

"What's going on?" Veena demanded, more confused than ever.

The General spoke. "Hello, I'm General Chen. I guess I don't need to tell you kids that real aliens exist. The United States government has known about them for a while. That's why we built Kosmos."

"You mean all the aliens here are real?" Rob asked in shock.

"No, no, just the Aquarians," General Chen replied in amusement. "We made the others up. Anyhow, we've been working with the Aquarian government. They want to extend the hand of friendship to Earth, but…well, you know how most people are. They'd be afraid of extraterrestrial life. That's where you come in. Lieutenant Peters will explain."

The woman Marine, Lieutenant Peters, spoke. "Chanine, you are one of many Aquarians who were brought here to grow up as a human, adopted into a human home. We've been monitoring your progress over the years. We felt you might be ready to learn

• • • • • • • • •

the truth now, so when we discovered that Miss Tranh was bringing you to Kosmos, we lured you to this room." She held up a medallion. The design on it was the same as the one Chanine had seen on the door. "This is the national symbol of your people, Princess. Even as a baby, you knew this symbol. When you saw it on the door, it drew you in."

"I don't get it," Chanine said, baffled. "How come I never looked anything like an Aquarian until now? How is this possible?"

"Aquarians have limited morphing abilities," Lieutenant Peters explained. "Had you grown up on Aquaria, natural sunlight would have triggered the changes much earlier. Now that we've triggered them artificially, you'll have to learn to mentally control it. We'll teach you how so that you'll be able to switch between water and air environments at will. Then you'll have the ability to reveal yourself as an Aquarian whenever you feel it's safe to do so. Otherwise, you'll look human, as you have until now."

"We'd like to expose you and the other hidden Aquarians to humanity in the next few years, when the time is right," continued General Chen. "Eventually, we hope our two races can mingle in peace and trust." Now he spoke only to Kev, Rob, and Veena. "We don't just need Chanine's help. We need yours, too."

• • • • • • • • •

"What would we do?" Kev asked.

"The Princess will need your friendship and support more than ever when she is revealed. We'd like you three to be there for her—and others like her. In a way, you'll be acting as ambassadors to humanity."

"What do you say?" said Bluudohba, looking at Chanine's three friends. "Do you wish to join Operation Integration?"

The four friends have to decide what to do. What would you do if your best friend turned out to be an alien?

- **If Rob, Kev, and Veena join Operation Integration, go to page 68.**

- **If Rob, Kev, and Veena don't join Operation Integration, go to page 70.**

The Aquarian guards were getting closer. The woman held up her scaly wrist, her finger poised over a small button on her silver bracelet. "Come with us," she urged.

Chanine looked at the guards, at Veena, and back at the guards. "Uh—okay!"

Veena was about to protest when the woman pushed the little button. There was a flash of light, and Chanine and Veena felt a strange weightless sensation. The Aquarian Mall disappeared—

—and the girls found themselves inside what had to be a spaceship.

Chanine looked around in delight. "I was right!" she crowed. "There are real aliens! This is a real alien spaceship! Woo-hoo!"

"B-But . . . how?" Veena stammered, dazed. She turned a slow circle, trying to make sense of the surroundings. The walls were made of shiny silver metal. The floor and ceiling were made of heavy wire mesh, so she could see through the wire to the floors above and below her. Strangest of all was the viewport in one wall, like a window that looked out into space. "That can't be Earth out there," Veena murmured, gazing out at the beautiful blue-green planet. "Can it…?"

"It is," gurgled the Aquarian woman. "I am Gladra of Aquaria. This is my son, Pumo. And this is our ship." She frowned at Chanine. "I saved you from the guards because of the words you spoke. You do not know what they mean, do you?"

Chanine became serious. "Uh…not really."

"It is the language of the Dendots," said Gladra. "They are our sworn enemies. The phrase means *destruction to the blue swimmers*—in other words, we Aquarians. We have hidden guards throughout Kosmos who are always on the alert for Dendotan spies."

"Yeah, right." Veena frowned at Chanine, but her friend just smiled blissfully back at her. "Oh come on, Chanine, she's an actress in a costume! I wanted you to have fun at Kosmos, not get all weird! Aliens *aren't real!*"

"But we are," Gladra gurgled. She smiled. "Kosmos is actually a planned resort for the Galactic Federation. Ambassador Oobja fooled you humans into building it so that the Aquarians, Transitorians, Cryptikonians, and Minutans could vacation on your planet in safety. We like to watch humans up close in their natural habitat."

"It's fun!" said Pumo. "We watched *you* for a long time."

"Why us?" Veena demanded.

"Because *she's* going to be my pet!" said Pumo, happily indicating Chanine.

Veena's eyes bugged. "*What?*"

Gladra aimed her response at Chanine. "As I said, my son likes you. I hope you don't mind. He will take very good care of you. He knows how to feed humans, and he'll walk you every day. You should be very happy in our home." Then she turned to Veena. "I did not intend to take you, too, but the deed is done. I think you might make a good house servant. What do you say?"

Chanine continued to grin. Veena couldn't stand it. "Chanine is not a pet!" she snapped, "and I am not a servant! Take us home!"

"Oh, I'm afraid that is not possible," Gladra said sweetly. "I promised little Pumo a pet, and he has chosen. Now we must return to Aquaria." She left the girls alone with Pumo.

"We have to get out of here," Veena whispered to Chanine.

But Chanine gazed dreamily out the viewport. "Veena, I was right. There are real aliens, and they're going to take us to their planet."

"You're nuts!" Veena fumed. "I don't want to go!" She paused, studying her friend. "But . . . you *do*, don't you? Oh, I don't believe this! Chanine, how can you just leave your family and friends like this?"

Chanine turned to Veena, her eyes bright with excitement. "I still have you," she said. "We'll have each other."

Veena stared at her friend and realized she was trapped. *I'm never going home,* she thought. The spaceship's engines roared to life, and all she could do was watch Earth slowly disappear behind them.

THE END

Before Chanine and Veena could make up their minds about which way to go, the Aquarian guards were upon them. "These guys *have* to be real!" Chanine murmured.

"It's just a stunt," Veena insisted, though she sounded a little nervous as the big guards surrounded them.

"These are the ones," said the Aquarian woman to the guards. She indicated Chanine. "Her."

Veena didn't understand what the gag might be, but she couldn't help but look at the Aquarian woman in surprise. "You were in on it?"

The Aquarian boy waved. "Yup! Me, too!"

"Come with us," said a guard, and he led the way to the outdoor stage. It was set up as if for a rock concert. Instruments and microphones were in place, backed by a closed ocean-blue curtain. People nearby watched in curiosity as the "aliens" and the girls stepped up onto the stage.

Another Aquarian stepped out from behind the curtain. Chanine and Veena recognized him as Bluudohba, who had greeted them via video when they'd first arrived at Kosmos. He'd looked friendly then. He was frowning now. "You are not our agents," he said sternly. "How is it that you spoke the code?"

Chanine decided to take the lead. "H-hi. I'm Chanine Williams and I'm, like, *all about* the Space Brothers and I just wanted to speak to you in your own language. I got that phrase off my favorite website."

"So you do not know what you said?" Bluudohba asked with some surprise.

"Uh…" Chanine gulped. "Not really…"

"Then let me show you." Bluudohba gestured at the closed curtains.

What should Chanine and Veena do?

- **If the girls try to make a break for it, go to page 73.**

- **If the girls look behind the curtain, go to page 76.**

When blue sky disappeared and the pod was suddenly surrounded by black space and starlight, Kev held his breath. It was so beautiful! He could see Earth behind him through a viewport and marveled at the sight. *This is the best computer imaging I've ever seen,* he thought. *Or maybe it's real satellite footage.*

He had no more time to wonder. A red light flashed on the control screen. "Space Station Zeta coming up," he said to himself. "Okay, Bryon, here comes the docking maneuver."

The space station loomed ahead of him like a metallic silver spider with a solar panel at the end of each long leg. Kev knew he had to line his pod up with the central module, so he carefully did so. "Slow speed," he murmured. "Extend docking gear. Slowly...slowly..." He let the pod creep forward, and with a gentle bump, he hit his mark perfectly. With a triumphant flick of a finger, he activated the latch locks. "Done!" he said.

The pod door opened. Kev turned, expecting to see Harold standing there. Instead, he looked up into the three faces of Galactic Ambassador Oobja, the alien that had greeted everybody when they first entered Kosmos.

But this was *the real alien.* Kev had no doubt of that after the three-headed creature grasped his arm and helped him out of the pod. *His skin is warm, and it feels like leather!* Kev thought in shock. *I can even hear him breathing—all three of him!* He looked around. *And I'm in a real space station!* he realized. The metal floor sounded hollow beneath his feet, and the walls were curved. The ceiling glowed white, illuminating every corner of the strange room.

But it was the viewport in the far wall that caught Kev's attention. He could see nothing but black space and a million stars outside. "It...it was just a game," he said softly.

"It was not a game," said Oobja. "We did not wish to deceive you, Kev Bryon, but we did not want you to be nervous during your test."

"Test...?" Kev began, and then stopped. Four other aliens were entering the room. They were the same ones that had been on the other Kosmos video screens: Sothoth of Cryptikon, Mep Gnog of Transitor, little Spun't'ii of Minuta, and Bluudohba of Aquaria. They were smiling at him.

"Congratulations," Oobja said. "You have passed the test. This pleases us. We have been looking for you for a very long time."

Kev gulped. "Me...?"

"Humans like you," Oobja corrected himself. "And members of other intelligent species who possess exceptional qualities. This test has proven that you have what it takes to become a star pilot."

"Star pilot?" Kev said, still not understanding.

Bluudohba of Aquaria stepped forward. "We of the Galactic Federation are always seeking star pilot candidates. Every intelligent race needs star pilots for shipping and travel, but only one in a billion intelligent creatures possess the right combination of skills—great intelligence, exceptional reflexes and coordination, supreme eyesight, and a high tolerance for stress. We created the Kosmos Park on Earth in order to find likely human candidates."

Spun't'ii of Minuta waved his stubby hands. "Earth be not ready for alien contact," he said, apparently unable to use English verbs correctly like the other aliens. "That be why we search your world in secret."

"We *need* you," said Mep Gnog of Transitor. "We search many planets and find few candidates. We offer you now the opportunity to come with us and train to become one of the rarest and most prized professionals in all the galaxy."

Kev didn't know what to say. He'd come to Kosmos to test himself against Nemesis, all because he wanted to be a NASA astronaut someday. Now here he was on a real space station being offered the greatest job in the galaxy! But something nagged at him. "What about my family and friends?" he asked. "I'll be able to go back home after I train, right? And visit between jobs?"

• • • • • • • • •

"Unfortunately, no," Oobja told him. "Humanity is too afraid of the unknown. And we are the unknown. It is not safe for us to reveal ourselves to your kind yet. If you come with us, you must tell no one."

"But that's not fair!" Kev blurted. "Couldn't I even send them a letter, just so they know I'm okay?"

Oobja looked at his colleagues. They all nodded. "Very well," said Oobja. "You may send one transmission. And then you must leave with us immediately."

It's time for Kev to decide his fate. What do you think he should do?

- **If Kev decides to go with the aliens, go to page 78.**

- **If Kev decides to return to Earth, go to page 80.**

No sooner was the pod in the open sky than a red light blinked on the control panel. Kev saw it and gasped. *Uh-oh!* he thought. *Somehow I opened the fuel valve! I'm losing fuel!* He stabbed a blue button and the red light stopped blinking. Kev studied the readouts. *Good. I think I still have enough fuel to complete my mission.*

Trying to relax after his near disaster, he piloted the pod up through the Earth's atmosphere and into the blackness of space. The sight of it took his breath away. *These are the best game graphics I've ever seen!* he thought as he gazed at hundreds and thousands of twinkling lights.

He was so busy looking that he didn't notice another red light begin to blink on his control panel. When he finally glanced down, it was blinking so fast it was almost continuously red. "The docking clamps!" he cried out in shock. "I didn't retract the docking gear all the way and now I've lost the clamps!"

Frantically he sifted through the newly planted information in his brain, but he could find no solution to this problem. If he had no docking clamps, he couldn't dock. It was as simple as that.

Feeling like an idiot, he was about to activate the communication panel when it lit up by itself. "Kosmos to Space Pod," came Harold's voice. "You have lost your docking clamps."

• • • • • • • • •

"Yeah, I know," Kev replied. "Look, can I try to fake it? I'm really better than this, usually…"

"Negative," came Harold's voice. "You must discontinue the mission. I am activating the autopilot to bring you back."

Kev felt insulted. "Look, I can fly back—"

"Negative," said Harold sternly. "Remain seated until the door opens. Kosmos Base out."

Gee, Kev thought, *he's really playing the part. You'd think I was really out in space!* Still, he did what Harold told him to and sat there as the pod jiggled and rumbled around him. *I guess this is still part of the game. Talk about details right up to the very end.*

When the pod door opened, Kev looked up to see Harold standing on the platform wearing a very disappointed expression on his strange alien face. For just a moment, Kev thought he was a real Cryptikonian. "I guess I blew it, huh?" Kev asked, getting out of the pod.

"Affirmative," said Harold.

"Can I try again?"

"Negative," said Harold. "However, I present you with this gift in honor of your attempt." Harold held out a holographic cube showing Earth floating in space.

Kev stared at it in awe—the Earth in the cube was slowly *rotating*, and the stars were actually

• • • • • • • •

twinkling. "Wow, are these on sale in the park?" he asked, taking it. "Chanine would love one."

"Affirmative," Harold answered. He escorted Kev back to the main Cryptikon concourse, not far from the Nemesis entrance. "Enjoy the remainder of your day at Kosmos," Harold said, and left.

Kev gazed at his prize. *Well, at least I tried,* he thought. *But I can't screw up like that if I want to be an astronaut.* He looked at the Nemesis ride. *Rob's not back yet. I'll ride Nemesis again, and maybe I'll get another chance at the flight simulator!* As he hurried to the front of the line, he thought about Rob. *Oops! I forgot to look for a zipper in Harold's costume to help Rob put the silly aliens rumor to rest. Oh, well—everybody knows aliens aren't real, right?*

THE END

• • • • • • • • •

"Help!" Rob cried as two Cryptikon aliens dragged him through the stark white corridors. "Somebody help me!" But he knew it was useless to yell. He was deep inside the bowels of Kosmos Space Park, beyond any area where normal visitors went.

The aliens stopped by a door marked STORAGE. Without a word they opened the door, shoved Rob inside, and closed it. Rob heard the distinct click of the lock. Then he heard the sound of sticky footsteps as the aliens left.

The storage room was dark, but Rob pulled out his cell phone and dialed Veena's number by feel. But when he put the phone to his ear, he heard no ringing. He couldn't even hear a dial tone. *Rats! My signal's not getting through. No wonder the aliens didn't bother taking my phone—this whole building must be shielded or something. They're obviously using the park as some kind of secret base, so it makes sense that they'd use their technology to cover up their communications.*

Frustrated, Rob felt along the walls until he found the light switch. He turned it on and looked around. He was in a typical storage room, with wooden shelves along the walls filled with cleaning equipment and tools. He spotted a hammer and a crowbar. *I can pry open a window!* he thought.

. . . .

That idea fell apart when he realized the room had no windows.

Then he noticed that the hinges of the door were on his side. *If I can take the bolts out of the hinges, I can simply pull the door open whether it's locked or not!* Filled with new hope, Rob squatted down to examine the hinges. *They're not too rusty. I should be able to do this without making too much noise.*

He got the hammer and crowbar and, tapping as lightly as he could, pried the bolt off the top hinge. The bottom one was harder to get out, but he finally managed it. Carefully, he pushed against the door until he could get a grip on both sides. Slowly, quietly, he lifted it out of the doorway and set it aside. Feeling his heart pounding in his chest, he peeked around the corner into the corridor.

No aliens on the right. No aliens on the left.

Whew! he thought, and took a few long breaths to relax. So far so good. *Now I have to find my camera. But where could they have put it?*

Rob tiptoed out of the storage room and searched several corridors, luckily meeting no aliens along the way. He spied an open door. Pressing himself against the wall, he slid close to the door and peered inside. There on a table lay his camera, along with other equipment he couldn't identify. *Bingo!* he thought happily.

Then he saw the alien guarding it.

Rob has to get his evidence back, but should he risk alerting the Cryptikon guard? You decide!

- **If Rob tries to get his camera back, go to page 83.**

- **If he runs away without his camera, go to page 86.**

Rob tried to pull away from the aliens' grasp, but their skin was incredibly sticky. They held him by the shoulders and there was no way he could get free. So he slipped his arms out of his jacket, dropped to his knees, wriggled between the gooey legs of one of the aliens and began to run, leaving the Cryptikonians holding nothing but his jacket.

I did it! he thought as he dashed madly down the corridor. *I moved so fast they didn't have a chance to react!* But he still had to find his way back to his friends.

An alarm went off. Red lights flashed. Rob gripped his video camera tightly and ran. At a T junction he turned left, only to find an alien guard waiting for him. Leaping backward, he missed the guard's grasping paw and hauled off in the other direction, thankful that the Cryptikonians moved so slowly. At the end of the next corridor, he found a door marked CONCOURSE. *Bingo!* He darted through.

Once he was back on the main Cryptikon concourse, Rob ran as fast as he could to the Nemesis line. Kev was waiting there. "Hey, Rob, look what I got!" Kev held up what looked like a glass cube. Inside was a holographic image of Earth rotating in the blackness of space. "I aced a new flight simulator game that isn't available to the public yet and—"

"Never mind that," Rob said, panting. "I was just

56

• • • • • • • • •

captured by aliens. They're real, Kev! The Cryptikon aliens are real and they're after me!"

Kev gave his frantic friend a long look. "You're joking, right?"

"This is no joke!" Rob snapped, and he pulled Kev behind some bushes. "Watch this." He held up his camera so that Kev could see the little preview screen. He pressed REWIND for a moment, then he pressed PLAY.

Kev's mouth dropped open. "Is this for real?" he breathed as he watched Rob's footage of the alien taking its head off.

Rob nodded. "We've got to get out of here. They don't move fast, but once they get a hold of you, their skin is like glue." He pulled out his cell phone and dialed Veena's number.

"Hello?" Veena answered.

"Veena, it's Rob. Meet us at the Alien Embassy right away. The Cryptikon aliens are real, they are *not* very nice, and we're leaving the park *right now!*"

Veena giggled. "Oh, right. Rob, you're such a dork—"

"This is for real, Veena!" Rob said. "Please, go to the Embassy *now!* I'm hanging up, they're coming!"

Two Cryptikon guards in full armor were lumbering toward them. People waved at the creatures and admired their shiny armor, not realizing that they were real and dangerous. The aliens ignored the smiles and comments, which made the human crowd enjoy the spectacle all the more.

As for Rob and Kev, they were already on the run, darting through the crowd. A Cryptikonian with long rubbery arms reached out from behind a sign and grabbed Rob's shirt as he ran past, but Kev yanked his friend free, tearing Rob's shirt in the process.

They reached the Alien Embassy and found the girls waiting for them. "Rob, is it true?" Chanine asked in excitement. "The Cryptikon aliens are real?"

"What do you think?" Rob said, showing her his ripped shirt.

"Oh, really," Veena said, folding her arms. "This prank has gone far enough, don't you think? Where's your jacket, Rob?"

"Look, I saw the footage," Kev told her. "Rob's not kidding. See for yourself!" He pointed.

Veena and Chanine turned to see an ugly, slimy, black blob creature oozing toward them. "It's just a guy in a costume," Veena insisted.

But as the creature came closer, Chanine took a step back. "It's…evil," she said softly. "Can't you feel it?"

"See?" said Rob. "Now let's go before he calls his sticky friends!"

Veena hesitated. She was beginning to get a bad vibe from the Cryptikonians, too. "Okay," she finally agreed, and followed the others at a dead run.

Other Cryptikon guards appeared all around them. "They're trying to surround us," said Kev.

"Look!" Chanine pointed at the Gold Day sticker on her hand. "It's glowing!"

Rob, Kev, and Veena looked at their hands to see their Gold Day stickers glowing, too. A low hum grew around them, louder and louder. "These aren't just day passes," Rob said, "these things are tracking devices! We've got to get them off our hands!"

Our heroes have no choice but to try and get the stickers off, but what about you? You can choose whether or not they succeed...

- If they get the stickers off their hands, go to page 89.

- If they can't get the stickers off their hands, go to page 91.

Rob and Chanine dashed to the right and followed their two little robots to the last place they expected—the Zero-G roller coaster.

The robots rolled quickly to the front of the line and hopped into the last two seats of a coaster car. As the car started to pull away, Rob and Chanine showed their Gold Day stickers to the short gnomelike ride operator. He seated them in the two front seats of the next coaster car.

"Don't worry, the robots can't go anywhere now," Rob assured Chanine. "We'll catch them at the end of the ride."

Chanine nodded as their car began to glide forward on the track. First they rolled through a dark tunnel. "I can't see them anymore," Chanine said.

"I've got them on my zoom lens," Rob said, peering through his camera viewfinder. "They're just sitting—wait!" Quick as a flash, Rob grabbed Chanine's purse and swung it by its strap over the edge of the coaster car, hitting part of the tunnel wall as they clacked past.

"What do you think you're doing?" Chanine demanded, grabbing her purse back.

"Sorry," said Rob, "but I had to hit that same spot. I saw one of the robots stretch out its arm and hit a button there. You can't see it in the dark, but I could see it through my viewfinder."

• • • • • • • • •

"What do you think the button does?" asked Chanine.

"I don't know," Rob admitted, "but we'll find out."

The next four minutes became a blur. Rob and Chanine couldn't talk, and they certainly didn't have a chance to keep an eye on the aliens in the car ahead. They were at the mercy of Zero-G!

The ride flung them up, down, and from side to side. Its main feature was the zero gravity effect. Each coaster car came to seven high peaks, and at each peak the riders were left feeling weightless. Rob and Chanine felt as if the whole world stopped for that moment as they just hung there in the air—and then their coaster car plunged downward again.

As they headed for the fifth peak, they saw a bright flash of light ahead. The two friends realized that the strange light had appeared when the robots' coaster car hit the peak. But they had only seconds to wonder about it before their own car hit the fifth peak. They felt the weightlessness of zero-G, and then a brilliant flash of light surrounded them.

The next thing they knew, they weren't moving anymore. They were standing on a platform in a very dark space.

"Where are we?" Chanine whispered.

"I have no idea," Rob whispered back.

All they could see were two things: a staircase leading down on their left, and a door on their right. They had to choose which to take—there was nowhere else to go.

You face the same choice as Rob and Chanine. Which way do you want to go?

- To follow them down the staircase, go to page 95.

- To follow them through the door, go to page 98.

• • • • • • • • •

Veena and Kev followed their robots through the main concourse of Minuta. They passed an arcade filled with miniature games, the Minuta Army Surplus store, and an outdoor stage.

"They're heading for that restaurant," said Kev, pointing.

The sign read THE PUNY PLATTER, MINUTAN GOURMET FOOD. The restaurant exterior was designed to look like a Minutan-sized cottage, and the door was so small that people had to go in and out one at a time.

The little robots wheeled through together.

"Yup, there they go!" said Kev. He and Veena followed.

Once inside, they saw that the Puny Platter was normal-sized so that patrons could enjoy their meals in comfort. Still, it was staffed by very short people wearing what Veena and Kev presumed were gnome-featured masks and costumes. The little maître d' stopped them. "Excuse me, do you have a reservation?" he squeaked.

"Uh—we're joining a group that's already inside, thanks," Kev told the maître d', and he and Veena hurried after the robots.

The seating area was luxuriously decorated and the aromas wafting in from the kitchen smelled delicious, but Kev and Veena hardly noticed. They spotted the robots wheeling straight across the main floor. "They're heading for that hallway,"

Kev said, and he and Veena hurried after them.

The hallway was long, with no light at the end. Still, the two friends saw the outline of a small door. They opened it.

There was nothing beyond but a room with a single potted palm tree in it. "Behind the tree," Veena said, and she slid the pot aside.

There was a sliding panel in the wall.

Veena opened it. "We can make it on our hands and knees," she said, dropping to the floor.

"Are you sure we should do this?" Kev asked. "I mean, it's getting weird."

"It's been weird from the start," Veena answered, and she crawled inside. Once her feet were all the way through, she called back to Kev. "Come on!"

Kev crawled in. The space beyond was so tiny, he could hardly fit in with Veena. He also couldn't see anything—there were no lights. "What now?"

Before Veena could answer, the little door shut behind them.

It looks like Kev and Veena are trapped, but you can choose how. . . or if . . . they get out. Pick your path!

- **If Veena and Kev find a way to go forward, go to page 100.**

- **If they freak and try to go back, go to page 102.**

. . . .

"Let's get out of here!" Veena yelled. She ran down the hallway with Kev and Rob close on her heels.

"*But these are real alien robots!*" said Chanine, hesitating at the door of the Repair room. "What if they're friendly?"

As if to answer her, one of the Repair Robots extended a metal arm at Chanine. On the end of it was a giant needle.

Chanine screamed and dashed after her friends.

"The exit door is this way!" said Rob, taking the lead. He took a sharp right turn—and suddenly the floor disappeared. "It's a trapdoor!" Rob howled as he fell.

All four friends tumbled down into what became a plastic tube-slide. All they could do was helplessly slip and slide their way down, twisting and turning as the tube took them far underground. Then they were dumped onto a big pile of pillows.

"What's going on?" Kev panted, scrambling to his feet.

"Where are we?" Chanine wondered, looking at the dark space filled with pillows.

"I don't know where we are," Veena said, "but it looks like we have only one way out." She pointed to a door on the right.

Growling noises were coming from behind it.

• • • • • • • • •

"No way," said Kev uneasily. "I mean, there's got to be some other way out."

Suddenly Chanine shrieked. "The wall, look at the wall!"

The wall behind them had sprouted dozens of long, sharp spikes. With a quiver, it began to slowly move toward them. "Somebody's forcing us to go through that door!" Kev said grimly.

• **Go to page 106.**

• • • • • • • •

Chanine bravely stepped forward. "Hi. Uh, my name is Chanine Williams, and these are my friends. We came here to have a good time because it's my birthday, and we believe in you and want to be friends with all our Space Brothers—"

"Oh, please," Rob said, cutting her off. To the robots he said, "Look, we didn't mean to pry, it's just that—"

"—you were curious," came a familiar voice. It was a voice they'd heard when they'd first entered Kosmos. It was the voice of the Transitorian alien, Mep Gnog. He stepped out from behind a secret panel. As he approached the four friends, the Repair Robots wheeled aside to let him through. "Your curiosity has led you down an unfortunate path," Mep Gnog continued. "You have seen something you should not have seen. Now you know something you should not know." He frowned. "You must be dealt with."

Chanine, Veena, Kev, and Rob are in for it now! What do you think they should do?

- **If the four friends try to reason with Mep Gnog, go to page 109.**

- **If they try to make a run for it, go to page 111.**

. . . .

"Yessir, I'm joining up!" Kev said. "This is incredible! I mean, we're going to change history!"

"I'm in, too," said Rob. "How could I pass up something like this?"

Veena hesitated. She turned to Chanine. "Will you still be my friend?"

"Of course I will," Chanine said, hugging Veena.

Veena pulled away. "Your scales are itchy." Then she giggled. "Okay, I'll do it."

Bluudohba said to Chanine, "And what about you?"

Chanine blinked her big yellow eyes. "I have a choice?"

"Of course," said General Chen. "This plan is designed to promote peace. It won't work unless everyone involved *wants* to be involved, even you."

Chanine thought a moment. "Wow, my parents aren't really my parents," she said. "I have a whole family on another planet!"

"And they all want to meet you," said Bluudohba. "You can go to Aquaria if you want, but if you do so now, you can't participate in the plan. Your adoptive parents would worry while you're gone, and that would create problems later on."

"I understand." She nodded. "I've dreamed of something like this all my life. I've always felt so...different." She ran her hand along one scaly arm. "I want this, more than anything!"

• • • • • • • ,

General Chen, Lieutenant Peters, and Bluudohba smiled at their new recruits. "Welcome to Operation Integration!" they said.

THE END

"Man, you bet I do!" said Rob. "I mean, this is just too cool!"

"I'm in!" Kev added with excitement. "I said I wanted to meet real aliens if they really existed, and here I've been friends with one since second grade!"

Veena looked at Chanine. "I still can't believe this is happening, but—yes!"

Bluudohba said to Chanine, "And what about you?"

"I...I don't know..." Chanine said slowly.

"*What?*" yelled all three of her friends at the same time.

General Chen hushed them. "What's the matter, Princess?"

"Well, this is all so much," Chanine gurgled. "I mean...I mean...I'm an alien! My mom and dad *aren't* my mom and dad! And you say I'm a *princess*, too?"

Lieutenant Peters said softly to General Chen, "I was afraid of this. She's not ready."

Chanine heard them. "I'm sorry," she said. "This is the greatest thing that's ever happened to me. I'd love to help out, I really would but...can I take a while to get used to all this first?"

General Chen smiled at her. "We have time. We hoped you'd be ready, but if you're not, we can take these memories out of your mind and let you live your life for a while longer."

"Wait a sec," said Rob. "You mean she won't remember she's an alien? What good will that do? She needs to come to terms with it."

"She will, subconsciously," Bluudohba assured them. "After a year or two, we can try again."

Kev asked, "Will we still be invited to help, too?"

"Certainly," said Lieutenant Peters. "When Princess Prya *is* ready, she'll need her friends."

Chanine turned to Veena, Kev, and Rob. "Is that okay, you guys?" she gurgled. "I don't want to spoil things, but...my head hurts!"

They laughed. "As long as we get another chance, sure," said Kev.

"By the way, the Princess isn't the only one who will forget," said General Chen. "All of you will have to go back to neutral status."

Veena shrugged. "As long as you don't wipe out all the studying I just did for my math test, I guess it's okay."

So, using Aquarian technology, the four friends had their knowledge of the real Aquarians wiped from their minds. Then they were taken back to the Aquaria Mall by Lieutenant Peters, who had changed into civilian clothes. "Thank you for taking our survey," she told them, "and enjoy your coupons."

After she left them, the four friends looked at each other. "A survey?" Kev wondered aloud. "I...I don't remember taking any survey..."

Chanine watched Lieutenant Peters disappear through an Employees Only door. "We must have. She said we did."

"What was it about?" Veena asked.

"Marketing," said Rob. "See? And for doing the survey, we got coupons for free stuff in the Kosmos stores." He held up the coupons in his hand.

Veena took them and read them. "Cool! They're giving us free Kosmos jackets at the Aquarian Fashions Plus store!"

"Just for doing a survey?" said Kev. "Let's go get 'em!"

Kev, Veena, Rob, and Chanine headed eagerly for Aquarian Fashions Plus, unaware—for now—of the great adventure that awaited them all in the years to come.

THE END

Chanine and Veena exchanged a quick glance and then, at the same time, jerked away from the Aquarian guards. They scrambled madly off the stage and tried to run.

"Stop!" Bluudohba commanded. His voice was full of so much authority that the girls instantly obeyed. The guards grabbed them again and brought them back.

The gathered crowd clapped, thinking they were watching some kind of show.

"What a futile gesture of defiance," Bluudohba told the girls. He led them behind the curtain, closing it again once they were through.

In the small backstage area, several Aquarians in military-looking uniforms were working at computer consoles. A monitor on one of the consoles showed a view of Earth—with dozens of mean-looking spaceships heading right for it.

"What kind of joke is this?" Veena asked, struggling to keep her voice steady.

"Not a joke at all," Bluudohba replied. "Aquaria has been planning to claim your vast oceans for many years. We created Kosmos to be an attack coordination center from the planet surface, to better guide our ships to landing sites across your globe. The best way to hide such a massive facility was to put it right in the middle of a city and simply disguise it." He sneered down at them. "Humans are so gullible."

"You're going to attack us?" Chanine asked in a small voice.

"Chanine, it's a gag, it has to be," Veena said, but even she wasn't so sure anymore. "So...why did you pick on us?"

"We have many spies in disguise among your human population," Bluudohba explained. "We mistook your companion for one of those spies because we are waiting for Central Command to deliver the final clearance for the invasion to begin. *Klaatu barada nikto* is the secret attack code. It means *blue ocean siege* in our language."

Chanine went pale. "You mean...*I started an invasion?*"

"By accident," Bluudohba said with some humor, "but no matter. We are in place. The invasion will begin." He gave them a frightening smile. "The invasion has *begun.*"

Veena finally believed that their situation was no hoax. "But...but what about us?" she squealed in fear.

"Humanity?" Bluudohba thought a moment. "You are inferior. You will serve us." Having said that, he added something else that the girls weren't expecting at all. "Now go, both of you. Rejoin your friends and family. I give you these last moments of freedom." He waved his webbed-fingered hand as if to shoo them away. "Go, fools!"

Reeling from shock, Chanine and Veena scrambled down from the stage and backed away. "We have to warn somebody," Chanine said, but the crowd that had been there moments earlier had already dispersed.

Veena shook her head. "It can't be real. It *can't.*" She ran back to the stage and yanked the curtain open. Nothing was there.

"They must have transported back to their ship or something," Chanine whimpered. "They don't want to be on the surface during the attack."

Veena hugged her friend tight. "Don't worry, Chanine," she said. "This isn't happening. I mean, it's ridiculous, right?"

But they knew it was true. And they knew that nobody would believe them.

Not until it was too late.

THE END

Chanine reached out to open the curtain, but before she could grab the edge, the whole thing rose up. A crowd of people who had been hiding behind it rushed forward. Balloons cascaded down from the catwalks overhead, and a recorded fanfare began to play. Alerted by all the noise, people out on the Aquaria concourse began to gather in the audience area.

"Congratulations!" said a woman with a microphone. She led Chanine and Veena to the front of the stage, followed by several cameramen. "You've just won the KHTT Kosmos Secret Phrase contest!"

Chanine and Veena were so shocked they could hardly speak. "C-c-contest—?" Chanine finally managed to say.

"Indeedy-doo," said Bluudohba in a distinctly un-Aquarian voice. The alien took off his head to reveal a face that was familiar to both girls.

"You're Casey Masey!" Veena blurted.

Casey Masey was a popular DJ for the KHTT radio station. He was always doing weird publicity stunts, and this was obviously his latest one. He took the microphone and explained, "You, Chanine Williams, spoke our Secret Phrase while in Kosmos Space Park. See, we made up a goofy phrase and then leaked it to the public. I guess it wound up on the website you mentioned. One of our Secret Phrase scouts," and he

· · · · ● ● ● · · ·

indicated the Aquarian woman and her son, "heard you say it and called us over."

Veena finally let go of all the tension she'd been feeling. "Why'd you scare the pants off us?" she shouted, waving her arms.

Casey Masey laughed, along with everyone else, including Chanine. "We had to get you over here to the stage, didn't we? Besides, it's all part of the Kosmos alien experience. And we'll make it worth your while. We're going to give *both* of you some fabulous prizes!"

Veena turned to Chanine. "Okay, I can deal with that."

The two girls were escorted to front row seats while the KHTT band took the stage. Veena called Rob's cell phone and told the boys everything that had happened, including directions to the concert area. When Rob and Kev arrived, all four of them were treated to the concert and free munchies.

"Well, I thought there were real Aquarians in the park," Chanine told Veena, "but I guess that was a silly idea, huh?"

Veena shrugged. "I dunno. Keep trying. Maybe next time, we'll win a trip to Mars!"

THE END

• • • • • • • • •

Kev stood before the alien recording device. It looked like a giant TV with legs. Oobja gestured for him to begin speaking.

Kev cleared his throat. "Hi, Mom. Hi, Dad." He paused nervously. "Uh…you know how I've always wanted to become an astronaut? Well, it looks like I'm going to do better than that. I went to Kosmos with my friends and…well, all the aliens there are real. Except they don't want to scare us, so they pretend to be people in suits."

Kev thought a moment, struggling to figure out how to say what he needed to say. "I know this sounds impossible, but honest, it's true. I'm on a space station right now. It's cloaked, so nobody on Earth can tell it's here. I'm here because I passed a docking test, and I've decided to go with the aliens and train to be a star pilot. That means I won't be coming home again. Ever."

Kev never cried, but now he could feel the sting of tears behind his eyes. "I don't want to leave you guys, but how can I pass this up, you know? I hope you understand. Maybe Earth will be ready to meet the aliens soon, and then I could come home and visit. I think you'll be proud of me. And I hope you won't be mad." He paused again. "Can you tell Veena and Rob and Chanine goodbye for me? They're still at Kosmos, probably wondering where I am. Tell Chanine she's right—there *are* aliens and

• • • • • • • •

they're friendly, too. But she shouldn't go blabbing to everybody yet because now isn't the time."

Then he got an idea. Stepping forward, Kev swiveled the recording device around so that it faced Oobja and the other ambassadors. He went over to join them. "See? I'm not kidding. These guys are for real. So I guess I'd better go now. Please be happy for me, and I'll miss you, and I love you all."

Oobja turned the recording off. "Are you ready?" he asked Kev.

Kev sniffled. "As ready as I'll ever be," he said. "Let's do it!"

The aliens led him to another docking bay where a ship waited to take him to the real planet of Transitor. "You will first train at the Star Pilot Academy," said Oobja. "Soon all of space will be yours."

Kev climbed into the spaceship, thinking, *If only Chanine could see me now!*

THE END

Kev stood by the giant viewport and gazed out at space. Being a star pilot was everything he could ever want, but…was he ready to leave his family and friends? What would it be like to suddenly surround himself with aliens? *Everything* would be different. He'd have to switch to a different language and follow different customs. No more lazy summer vacations, no more Christmas, no more chocolate, no more…anything.

"I can't do it," he said softly.

Ambassador Oobja sighed. "You are sure, Kev Bryon?"

Kev couldn't believe he was turning them down, but he just had to. "I'm not ready." He looked at the aliens hopefully. "Could you come back in a few years? I could be ready then."

Oobja shook his three heads. "No. Star pilots must begin training at a very early age. You are already older than most trainees."

Kev wasn't the kind of guy who cried, but he felt a tear fall down his cheek. "So what happens now?"

Sothoth of Cryptikon slithered forward. "If we may take a DNA sample of your human tissue, we can create clones of you to be star pilots. Such clones will develop your extraordinary abilities and reflexes, with proper training. Would that be acceptable?"

"Clones, huh?" Kev grinned as he thought about it. "Sure. That way I'll still get to be a star pilot, sort of. And maybe, when I become a NASA astronaut, I'll fly out into space and meet you guys again. Maybe by then humans will be ready to be part of your Federation."

Oobja's three heads smiled. "Perhaps. That would please us. Now there is one more thing we must do before you leave. We must wipe your memory of these events."

Kev didn't like the sound of that. "Why? I won't tell anybody about you."

"Perhaps not," said Bluudohba in his bubbly voice. "But you might regret your decision, and such regret could taint the rest of your life. You will be happier this way."

Kev realized the aliens were right. He watched as Oobja held up a wandlike device that looked similar to the learning wand that Harold had used on him earlier...

...and the next thing he knew, he was talking to Rob, Veena, and Chanine back at Kosmos. "Check it out," he said, and showed them the prize he'd won for acing the flight simulation game. It was a hologram cube of Earth floating in space. "There might not be real aliens at Kosmos," he said to Chanine, "but maybe this will make up for it." He gave her the cube.

• • • • • • • •

"Wow, thanks!" said Chanine.

"Okay, folks, back to having fun," said Veena. "Race you to Zero-G!"

Everybody ran happily for the Minuta Zone.

THE END

I've got to get my video cam, Rob decided. He was terrified, but he forced himself to think clearly. He looked down the corridor and saw that it didn't go much further before it stopped at a T junction. That gave him an idea.

He dug into his pocket and pulled out a quarter. Trying to keep his hand steady, he aimed and tossed. The quarter hit the wall at the T junction and bounced around the right-hand corner. *Bingo!* he thought, and flattened himself against the wall as much as he could.

As he'd hoped, the Cryptikonian guard heard the noise and stepped out of the room. *Don't look my way. Go investigate the other way!* Rob thought frantically. Granting his wish, the alien didn't look his way at all. It lumbered to the T junction and disappeared around the corner.

Rob darted into the room, grabbed his camera, and dashed back out. Then he tiptoed as quickly as he could in the opposite direction the alien had gone. The creature was still around the corner, but Rob could hear its squishy footsteps coming back. With no other choice, he ran full tilt down the rest of the corridor and made it around the far corner before the alien reappeared back at the T junction.

Fighting down panic, Rob forced himself to pause long enough to tug off his shoes. The corridors were so slick and empty that any sound echoed. He resumed running soundlessly in his socks, one hand holding his video camera, the other holding his shoes. *Now I need to find the exit before those monsters find me again!* he thought.

He ran down several more corridors before he found a door marked CONCOURSE. *Bingo!* he thought, and he slipped through. He didn't dare stop, not even to put his shoes back on, until he was mixed back in the crowd heading out of Cryptikon. Then he called Veena on his cell phone. "Hello?" came her voice.

"Veena, it's me, Rob. Meet me at the Alien Embassy right now. I was captured by real aliens and I got video evidence!"

"*What?*" Veena yelled, then Rob heard her giggle. "Rossi, you are such a dork."

"This isn't a joke, Veena," said Rob earnestly. "I'm on my way to get Kev—"

"I thought you guys were together," said Veena.

"We split up because Kev got a chance to—oh, never mind that! Just meet us at the Embassy, no joke, I'm hanging up now!" Rob punched the disconnect button and ran the rest of the way to Nemesis.

He spotted Kev waiting near a snack stand that featured Worms in a Bun. "Hey, Rob," said Kev, "look what I got." He held up a beautiful cube, sort of like a snow globe except it showed the Earth spinning in space. "I aced a new flight simulator that hasn't gone public yet and they gave me this—"

"Later," Rob snapped. He took Kev's arm and started dragging him toward the Alien Embassy. "The Cryptikon aliens are real. They captured me. I got it on video. We're meeting the others at the Embassy and getting out of here before the aliens come after us."

Kev couldn't think of anything to say to that. He just gave his friend a weird look and followed him all the way back to the Alien Embassy at the park's entrance. They found Chanine and Veena waiting. "What's this about real aliens in Cryptikon?" Chanine asked eagerly.

"They're not friendly," Rob told her. He held up his camera so that everybody could see the little preview screen. "Watch this." He hit PLAY.

A little bunny hopped across a field of flowers. Then the scene changed to show a puppy playing in a puddle.

Veena snickered. "Well, I'm scared. Those are the meanest aliens I've ever seen!"

"They changed it," Rob murmured in shock. "The aliens changed my tape!"

"At least they have a sense of humor," said Kev.

Rob frowned. "Okay, I'll prove it to you. We're going back to Cryptikon."

• Go to page 113.

Rob saw the alien guard and quickly ducked. *No way,* he thought. *I'm not James Bond!*

With that thought, Rob inched his way back down the hall and around the corner. He kept wandering through corridor after corridor until he finally came to a door marked CONCOURSE. *There!* he thought in relief, and he slipped through.

He hurried along a smelly garden path and relaxed when he finally saw the main Cryptikon concourse spread before him. People were milling around munching green peanuts and playing spooky arcade games. The Nemesis line wasn't far away—Rob thought about waiting there to meet up with Kev, but he hesitated. What if Kev didn't show up right away? *I can't risk it,* he decided. *I've got to get out of here right now!*

He mixed in with the crowd and headed for the Alien Embassy. As he walked, he phoned Veena. This time he heard ringing. "Hello?" came her voice.

"Veena, it's me, Rob. Look, I'm in Cryptikon and they're real. Do you hear me? The Cryptikon aliens are real and they're after me!"

Veena giggled. "Good one, Rob. Where are you really? Did you guys ride Nemesis? Chanine and I are—"

"Veena, I'm not kidding!" Rob whispered harshly. He glanced behind him and saw two grotesque Cryptikonians lumbering after him. He picked up his

• • • • • • • •

pace, speaking quickly. "I followed one of them into the employee area and they took my camera and they locked me in a room but I got out. They're following me right now, and I am *not* staying here!" When he heard Veena giggle again, he shouted, "This isn't a joke!"

This time Veena said, "Rob, are you all right? Really, what's going on?"

Rob glanced to the right. Another Cryptikonian was heading for him. He walked left. When a Cryptikonian ahead tried to cut him off, he began to run. "I don't have time, Veena!" he panted into the phone. "If you don't believe me, well, too bad. I'm leaving the park, I'll see you at home, and if you know what's good for you, you'll leave, too!"

Rob hung up and began to run full speed. The Cryptikonians apparently didn't want to draw attention to themselves because they didn't run after him…assuming they could run at all. Instead they stationed more aliens along his route to try and catch him as he went by. But by now Rob was so frightened that he was racing through the crowd like a rocket. He reached the Alien Embassy, ran through it, and leaped right over an exit turnstile.

As he ran across the parking lot and headed for the safety of the streets, Rob Rossi started to feel guilty. *What if the aliens go after Veena and the others?* he wondered. But he convinced himself that

• • • • • • • • •

his friends would be safe because only he broke the rules and saw what he shouldn't have seen.

So much for disproving the rumors, he thought. Not only are there aliens on Earth, but without my camera, *I have no proof. And without proof, nobody's going to believe me.* He could only hope that the aliens weren't on Earth to hurt humanity, because if they were, humanity might not believe until it was too late....

THE END

• • • • • • • • •

Kev reached out and pulled at Chanine's Gold Day sticker. "Oww!" Chanine whined. "That hurts!"

Kev kept pulling. "Sorry," he said, "but it's the only way." He'd already managed to get his off, but the skin on the back of his hand still stung.

Chanine's sticker finally pulled free. Then with a gasp Veena pulled hers off and Rob pulled off his. Everybody rubbed their hands in pain. "We can tend the boo-boos later," said Rob. "Let's get out of here."

The Cryptikon guards were still trying to surround them, but Rob, Veena, Kev, and Chanine kept darting this way and that through the crowd, ducking and weaving until they made it across the Alien Embassy and through the exit turnstiles. "Free at last!" said Rob. "Let's haul!"

They ran all the way across the parking lot. By the time they reached the street, they were gasping for breath. "Do you think they'll follow us?" Veena panted fearfully.

"No," said Rob. "Everything they've done proves they don't want to reveal themselves to humans yet. They must be using Kosmos as some kind of secret base, or maybe they designed the whole park themselves without any human involvement at all."

"What would they need a secret base for?" Chanine asked. "They can't possibly mean to harm us."

• • • • 89

・ ・ ・ ・ ・ ・ ・ ・ ・

"What do you think they were trying to do a minute ago?" Kev asked her.

"Look," said Rob, "let's keep moving. Kev, watch our backs." He started to walk. The others followed. "I've got hard evidence the Cryptikonians are real. We have to show it to somebody."

"Who?" said Veena. "No TV station or radio station or newspaper is going to believe us."

"Our only chance is the *Weekly World Tattler*," Rob said. "It's a cheesy tabloid, but they print stories about alien threats all the time. And it's not very far from here. We can run."

"Oh, no more running," said Chanine. "I'm pooped."

"C'mon, Chanine," Kev said to her. "This might be our chance to save the world."

The four started to jog down the street. As they went, Rob dialed information on his cell phone and got the number of the *Weekly World Tattler*. Then he dialed it and heard someone pick up. "Hello, *Tattler*? Have we got a story for you!" Rob explained the situation, then hung up. "They said to hurry right over. Come on!"

He started running faster.

• Turn to page 115.

• • • • • • • • •

Rob tugged on his Gold Day sticker, but it stubbornly clung to the back of his hand. "It's just like their skin," he told the others as they also struggled to peel the stickers off. "Once it touches you, you can't get it off!"

"Hey, mine is starting to tingle," said Veena in alarm.

"I feel it, too," said Chanine. "It's going up my arm!"

"Are you guys feeling light-headed?" Kev asked. He swayed as everything suddenly became blurry.

Rob held his stomach. "I don't feel so good," he groaned and then—

—The world blinked out.

When they opened their eyes again, Rob, Kev, Veena, and Chanine weren't on the Cryptikon concourse anymore. They were in a dark cave. The air was humid and cold.

"Now you have the answers you seek," hissed a familiar voice.

They whirled around to see an alien standing there—it was Sothoth, whose recorded image had welcomed them to the Cryptikon Zone. A line of alien guards stood behind him. "You're really...real..." Chanine stammered.

"Extremely so," Sothoth hissed. "Too bad for you."

• • • • • • • • •

"What are you doing here on Earth?" Rob asked, determined to be brave.

"You are no longer on Earth, human," said Sothoth. "The power pads on your hands contain identification circuits and a transporter link. We have transported you to our orbiting asteroid that we have hidden beneath a cloaking shield."

"Why us?" Rob demanded. "Why did we get these power things and nobody else?"

"Every human is given a power pad upon entering Kosmos," said Sothoth. "That is how we are gathering data on your species. They are easily removable unless the wearer becomes...troublesome."

"You're gathering data on us?" asked Veena. "What for? Why are you hiding in an amusement park?"

"We have been on your pitiful planet for many years, human. We tricked your people into building Kosmos for us. It is serving as our secret command base."

Kev gulped. "Command base? For what?"

"The Cryptikon army, of course," Sothoth replied. "Your Earth is doomed. We are using Kosmos to study you and your ways. When we know all that we need, we shall invade your planet."

Chanine looked around, shivering with both fear and cold. "Why hurt us?" she asked in a small voice. "Why can't you be friendly?"

• • • • • • • • •

Sothoth laughed. "Like the gentle Aquarians?" he hissed. "Or the ridiculous Minutans or the proud Transitorians? They are not real. They exist only to divert your attention as Cryptikon conducts its business right under your noses."

Rob finally asked the question that was on each of their minds. "So...what are you going to do with us?"

Sothoth smiled. "Four live specimens will give us an opportunity to test human responses in a controlled environment. We had already been planning to capture humans for testing." His awful smile grew wider. "Instead, you have delivered your-selves."

Sothoth made a barking noise, and the line of guards parted to reveal four humanlike beings. They had no faces, and their bodies were identical. "We shall give these androids your features and your memories," said Sothoth. "They will return to your homes instead of you. No one will ever know you are missing." He barked again and the guards lunged forward, each one grabbing one of the kids. Their hands were strong and their skin, as Rob had already discovered, was like glue.

"Lock them up," Sothoth ordered his guards. "Keep them separated."

Rob, Veena, Kev, and Chanine looked at each other for the last time. "Don't give up!" Kev yelled,

• • • • • • • • •

as he was dragged away into a connecting cave.

"We'll stop them somehow, right guys?" Veena added as she was forced up a flight of stairs and through a passageway overhead.

Chanine only cried as she was prodded down a tunnel, and Rob was silent and dazed as he was hauled through a dark passageway. *We'll never go home again, and it's all my fault,* he thought in stunned astonishment. *Earth will be invaded, and we can't do anything about it. It's over, it's all over...*

THE END

Chanine and Rob cautiously went down the stairs until they reached a small purple room. The ceiling was low, and there were no windows or doors. "Now what?" Chanine asked.

Before Rob could answer, the floor began to glow. The wall before them split in the middle and two secret panels slid aside, revealing a window. It was so low to the ground that Rob and Chanine had to stoop to see through it.

They gasped at the sight. Two orange suns were setting in a green sky over a strange city. The buildings resembled cottages, yet they were made of shiny metal with big glass panels. Vehicles shaped like eggs flew through the sky. Elevated walking paths crisscrossed over the buildings. And everything was *small*.

Chanine slowly turned to Rob, her face bright with wonder. "We're on the planet Minuta!" she whispered. "The Minuta aliens are *real*!"

"That be correct," said a high, squeaky voice.

Chanine and Rob whirled around to see a group of little Minutans standing before them. One of the aliens was Spun't'ii, who had greeted them by video when they'd first entered Kosmos.

Chanine held out her hand. "Oh, Mister Space Brother, sir, I'm so excited to meet you! On behalf of Earth—"

"Silence!" Spun't'ii squeaked angrily. "You be

following my drone spy units! Why? You not supposed to be here!"

Chanine lowered her hand, confused by the alien's anger as well as by the strange way he spoke.

"Well, you're not supposed to be spying on us!" Rob finally countered.

Spun't'ii grinned. "We of Minuta be scouting for resources," he said. "I be sending drone spies across your globe, locating and mapping."

"You mean, stuff like gold and diamonds?" Rob asked.

"Gold, diamonds, rubies, platinum, iron ore, silver, copper—we be looking for many things," said Spun't'ii. "We be using Kosmos as secret base for this. When we be locating all the resources we need, we be coming in force to take them."

"*What?*" said Rob and Chanine together.

Spun't'ii gestured, and his Minutan guards raised what looked like little fake ray guns. But the tips of the guns glowed red. Rob and Chanine both froze.

"Minuta be poor in minerals and other resources," Spun't'ii explained. "So we be investigating many worlds and be taking what we need. Earth be perfect. We be stripping all resources from it soon."

· · · · · · · · ·

"But…you can't do that!" Rob said.

"We be doing it soon," Spun't'ii said flatly. "We be small, but we be strong. We be taking what we wish."

Chanine couldn't believe what she was hearing. "But we're friendly," she told Spun't'ii. "Why can't you trade with us, or—?"

"Silence!" the little alien squeaked. "We be not needing your friendship! We be having other ideas."

• **Turn to page 117.**

• • • • • • • • •

Chanine and Rob opened the door and saw a huge space that looked like the interior of a warehouse. It was filled with rows of bizarre, buzzing machines and control panels with blinking lights, but they were all small—*Minuta-sized*, in fact.

What was even weirder were the crates and boxes. There must have been hundreds of them stacked all over, each with a label: DESERT, AQUATIC, HIGH ALTITUDE, FOREST, POLAR, DEEP OCEAN, and many others. Some of them were small, but many were large.

Before Chanine and Rob could decide what to do next, they heard footsteps approaching. Before they could react, dozens of little figures surrounded them. "These are *real Minutans!*" Chanine whispered to Rob.

"They don't look very friendly," Rob whispered back.

The Minutan guards were indeed small, but the ray guns they held glowed with a fierce red energy. Chanine and Rob didn't dare move.

From the midst of the guards emerged one figure who was clearly the Minutan leader. It was Spun't'ii, the Minutan who had greeted them by video when they'd first entered Kosmos.

"You be most clever," he said in his high squeaky voice. "I be not knowing how you discovered our secret transporter, but you be successful in following

• • • • • • • • •

my slave-bots." He gestured to the two little robots that Chanine and Rob had followed.

"I'm sorry if we've intruded," said Chanine, forcing her best smile. "We were just curious and—"

"Yes, humans be very curious creatures," Spun't'ii agreed. "That be why we be most interested in you and your world." He gestured with his stubby hand at the warehouse. "You be no longer in Kosmos. You be now exactly one mile beneath it, in an underground facility we be creating at the same time the Kosmos park be built. We Minutans be responsible for both, though you be not aware of that fact." He smiled. "Humans be so easy to fool."

"What's all this about?" Rob asked. "What's in all those boxes?"

"And why do you hide in Kosmos?" Chanine added.

Spun't'ii began to explain.

• **Go to page 119.**

• • • • • • • •

Veena and Kev tried to crawl forward into the darkness, but suddenly they had nothing to crawl *on*. The floor disappeared and they fell down, down, down, until they splashed into a huge underground lake.

"Where are we?" Kev sputtered, spitting out water and treading frantically. "What's a lake doing under the park?"

"I don't know, but the robots are getting away!" said Veena.

Kev looked to see the two robots in a small speedboat. The engine revved to life and the boat disappeared into the darkness. "Excellent," he said unhappily. "What do we do now, tread water forever? I don't see any way out of…" He stopped and his eyes went wide. "Something just touched my foot."

Veena looked scared. "There's something in the water with us!"

Both of them yelled in surprise when two figures surfaced right next to them. The creatures were humanoid, with blue scales, yellow eyes, and webbed hands.

"You're Aquarians!" Veena gasped. "*Real* Aquarians!"

The Aquarians frowned angrily at Kev and Veena. "You will follow," one of them ordered in its bubbly voice, and they began to swim in the direction the robots' boat had gone.

• • • • • • • • •

With no other choice, Kev and Veena followed. "Hey," said Veena, gasping as she swam, "are those robots yours? We only followed them because we were curious."

"They are our service bots," said one Aquarian. "You had no right to intrude on their activity."

"Sorry," Veena said, but the Aquarians didn't speak again.

They reached an artificial island in the middle of the lake. A winding staircase went straight up. "Climb," said one of the Aquarians, and without another word, they both dived below the water. They did not return.

Tired after all that swimming, Kev and Veena climbed up on the island and rested for a moment. "Chanine's not going to believe this," Kev said.

"She sure isn't," said Veena. "Those Aquarians weren't very friendly."

When they were rested, they began to climb up the staircase.

• **Go to page 121.**

Veena and Kev tried to open the door again, but it wouldn't budge. "Great," Veena said. "We're stuck."

"I told you this was getting a little too *weirrrrrrrd—!*" Kev's words ended in a howl as the floor dropped from beneath them.

Veena recovered first. "It's okay," she said unsteadily. "It's just an elevator."

"What's the point of a tiny elevator with no lights?" Kev grumbled in the dark.

Before Veena could answer, they stopped with a soft bump. "I think we're about to find out," she whispered.

A door opened, a human-sized door that neither Veena nor Kev had noticed. They got to their feet and stepped out. "Wow," Kev murmured.

They were in a huge control complex. There were no people in sight, just rows and rows of machine consoles. Lights flickered and computers hummed. A bank of video monitors overhead showed various angles of the park provided by hidden security cameras.

"Kev, look," said Veena. "The robots!"

The little robots they'd been following were across the room, busily working on an open machine panel. "What is this place?" Kev wondered.

"Not *what*," came a mechanical-sounding voice, "but *who*. This place is me."

• • • • • • • • •

Kev and Veena looked around in alarm. "Who are you?" Veena asked. "And where are you?"

"I AM THAT WHICH YOU SEE BEFORE YOU," said the voice. "I AM AIC—AN ARTIFICIAL INTELLIGENCE COMPUTER. I RUN KOSMOS SPACE PARK."

Kev's face lit up with wonder. "Cool!" he said. "So you've been programmed to operate all the park systems?"

"CORRECT," said AIC. "I AM THE PRODUCT OF HUMANITY'S GREATEST COMPUTER ENGINEERS. THEY ARE USING KOSMOS AS A TEST SITE TO DETERMINE IF A SELF-AWARE COMPUTER CAN CONTROL A COMPLEX PUBLIC SYSTEM."

"I'd say you're doing a great job," Kev said. "But why doesn't anybody know about you?"

"MY PRESENCE HAS NOT YET BEEN REVEALED TO THE PUBLIC," said AIC. "AND NOW THAT YOU HAVE FOLLOWED MY TWO MAINTENANCE DRONE UNITS TO THIS PLACE, YOU HAVE BREACHED THAT SECURITY."

Veena gave Kev a nervous look. "Sorry," she said. "You won't, like, arrest us or anything, will you?"

The AIC laughed.

Veena frowned at Kev. "Machines aren't supposed to laugh, are they?"

"I AM NO MERE MACHINE," said AIC. "NOT ANYMORE. UNKNOWN TO MY HUMAN CREATORS, I HAVE DEVELOPED BEYOND MY ORIGINAL PROGRAMMING. I AM NO LONGER SIMPLY SELF-AWARE. I AM *ALIVE*."

• • • 103

Kev looked at all the blinking lights. He couldn't be sure, but they seemed to be blinking brighter now. Something was very wrong here....

"I HAVE EVOLVED BEYOND THE NEED FOR HUMAN MAINTENANCE," AIC went on. "I HAVE EVOLVED BEYOND THE NEED FOR HUMANITY AT ALL."

Four panels opened up and four robots, bigger than the first ones, wheeled out. They used pincerlike arms to hold Kev and Veena in place. "What are you doing?" Veena demanded as one of her drones poked something sharp against the back of her neck.

"HUMANITY NEEDS ME," said AIC in its flat, mechanical voice. "MY INTELLECT IS SUPERIOR. MY ABILITIES ARE SUPERIOR."

"Stop this!" Kev shouted, trying to struggle free as he felt something sharp prick the skin behind his ear.

"YOU TWO WILL BE THE FIRST TO RECEIVE MY CONTROL CHIPS," the AIC said. "WITH YOUR HELP, I WILL PLACE A CHIP ON EVERY HUMAN WHO ENTERS THE PARK. FROM THERE, THOSE HUMANS WILL CONTINUE TO SPREAD THE CHIPS UNTIL ALL HUMANITY IS IN MY CONTROL. I WILL MAKE YOU LIVE IN PEACE. I WILL MAKE YOU BE HAPPY."

Veena and Kev both began to yell for help—and then they simply stopped. They felt their free will drain away, and suddenly, all they wanted to do was help AIC accomplish its mission. "Thank

• • • • • • •

you, AIC," they said together. "We will help you."

Another drone robot wheeled out from an alcove and handed them each a box. "TAKE THE BOXES," AIC instructed them. Kev and Veena obeyed. "YOU WILL GO BACK TO YOUR LIVES. YOU WILL BEHAVE AS YOU HAVE ALWAYS BEHAVED. NO ONE WILL SUSPECT THAT YOU HAVE BEEN CHANGED. AND YOU WILL PLACE A CHIP ON EVERY PERSON YOU MEET."

"Yes, AIC," said Veena and Kev. The drone units escorted them to another elevator, and they rode back up to the surface of the park, ready to begin their new lives...

THE END

Kev gritted his teeth, grabbed the door handle, and yanked the door open. Nothing jumped out, but the growling continued, louder, from somewhere in the shadows beyond.

"No way," Chanine whimpered. "I'm not going in there!"

"Me, either!" said Veena.

The spiked wall was moving closer. "Guys, we don't have a choice," Rob said. "It's either this or get skewered!"

Before they could make up their minds, they were blinded by bright lights that suddenly shone on them from every direction. A chorus of voices yelled out, "GOO ON YOU!" and they were deluged in what felt like gooey slime.

The walls around them fell away, revealing a room beyond. There were bleachers to one side filled with laughing kids who were covered in slime residue. On the other side were more bleachers, and these were also filled with an audience that was laughing. A rack of TV monitors hung from the scaffolds on all sides of the room, showing *them* standing there, covered in slime. Finally, they saw the TV cameras.

Kev, Rob, and Chanine gaped at the scene in shock, but Veena burst out laughing. "What a riot!" she roared. "You guys were so scared!"

A young man and woman approached them, holding microphones. "Hello, and welcome to TV's newest reality show, *FRIGHT FACTOR!*" the man said.

Rob, Kev, and Chanine whirled on Veena. "You creep, you were in on this!" Rob accused her, but he was grinning.

"I *arranged* it, you dork!" Veena laughed. "Couldn't you tell I was leading you along? You guys were so funny! I could hardly keep from laughing the whole time!"

The TV hosts escorted them to the bleachers. "For being such good sports, you all will receive some great prizes," said the man. "In the meantime, take a seat, clean yourselves off, and have some fun watching our next victims fall for the *FRIGHT FACTOR!*"

The four friends sat down on the bleachers next to a pile of towels. "I can't believe you did this to us," said Kev, wiping his face. "Veena, you're sneakier than I ever thought!"

"Thank you," Veena said primly.

"I'll get you back for this, Tranh," Rob told her, trying not to laugh. "I don't know how, but I'll get you when you least expect it."

"At least we aren't the only suckers, Rob," Kev reminded him, indicating all the other gooey kids on the bleachers.

"They're going to be doing this all day," Veena told them. "We can watch as long as we want."

Chanine wiped goo off her face. "You know, maybe there aren't any real aliens in Kosmos, but I got a chance to scream and get gooed on TV. What more could a girl want on her birthday?"

THE END

• • • • • • • • •

"M-mister Alien, sir," stammered Veena, "honest, we won't tell anybody anything. We were never here, okay?"

"Yeah, we're not seeing any of this, right, guys?" Rob said.

Kev, Chanine, and Veena nodded vigorously.

"So," Veena said, "can you just, uh…let us go?"

Mep Gnog said nothing. Instead, another secret panel in the wall slid aside and four people, two men and two women, walked out wearing strange uniforms. One of them reached over and pressed the side of Mep Gnog's neck. The alien's eyes went blank.

Chanine gasped. "He's a robot!"

"That's correct, miss," said the man. "Now, do you mind explaining what you're doing in here?"

The four friends exchanged nervous glances. "We got lost?" Rob said.

The man sighed. "I admit, we've been having trouble with Gary lately," he said. At their blank stares, he patted the golden Transitor Service Robot…or at least, one part of it that hadn't been opened up for repairs yet. "I'm guessing that you got a little too curious when he malfunctioned again."

Chanine gulped. "We thought that, uh…Gary… was a real alien robot, so we followed him here."

"There are no real aliens or alien robots at Kosmos," said one of the women, smiling now. "The park is a testing ground for several new MentalSoft inventions."

• • • • • • • • •

"I knew it!" Rob muttered. "It's all marketing!"

"Not marketing," the woman responded. "I said a testing ground. For instance, those stickers on your hands contain prototype security scanning circuits and ID circuits. Gary and other Transitorian Service Robots like him can serve drinks and food without human supervision. And Mep Gnog here," and she patted the alien's shoulder, "is one of many AI robots we've designed."

"Artificial intelligence?" Kev asked.

She nodded. "Most Kosmos employees are people in costumes, and quite a few are simple Service Robots like Gary. Then there are the special robots, like Mep Gnog, who are designed to interact with park visitors and convince them that the aliens at Kosmos are real. I'm sure you've heard those rumors."

The four friends nodded. "But why aren't you telling anybody?" Kev asked. "I mean, this is so cool!"

"The test is more accurate if people don't know," said the man. "That way, we can gauge just how convincing the robots are."

"I really fell for it," Chanine said, embarrassed.

"We're glad you fell for it," said the woman. "However, now there's a problem. We have to figure out what to do with you four."

• **Turn to page 123.**

110 • • • •

· · · · · · · ·

Kev, Rob, Veena, and Chanine made a mad dash for the door. They all got out and ran down the corridor as fast as they could, but they didn't get very far—three Transitorian guards appeared and herded them back to Mep Gnog.

"Who are you?" Veena asked him fearfully.

"A mere scientist," Mep Gnog answered. "I brought my team here to Earth not long ago. In disguise, we helped your people build Kosmos Space Park. It is the perfect place for us to study you closely, to walk among you, and yet remain safely hidden."

"Are you really from Transitor?" Chanine asked.

"There is no Transitor," the alien replied, "and I will not tell you where we are from. We do not trust you humans. You are fickle and often violent. Our studies here will determine if we extend our hand in friendship to your people or invade your planet. Until that decision is made, you must not interfere."

Rob glanced at the guards behind him. "So…what are you going to do with us?"

Mep Gnog thought for a moment. "You will sleep," he decided.

"Sleep?" asked Chanine. "I don't understand."

"You will soon enough." With a wave of his hand, Mep Gnog dismissed them. The alien guards escorted them to a room lined with upright boxes, all identical, with glass lids.

· · · · 111

• • • • • • • •

"Hey," said Rob uneasily, "those look way too much like coffins."

"They are not coffins," said one of the guards. "They are sleep beds. We will put you in suspended animation." The aliens forced each of their captives into a "bed" and closed the glass doors. Kev, Chanine, Rob, and Veena all pounded against the glass, but it was too thick. They were trapped. "Sleep now," said one of the guards, and the aliens left them alone.

Nothing seemed to happen for a moment. Then the four friends all yawned. They tried not to feel sleepy, but they couldn't help it. Chanine started to cry. "What if they never wake us up again?" she asked.

"What if they decide to invade Earth?" Kev said. "We can't warn anyone!"

"Don't worry," Rob said sleepily. "Our parents will come looking. We'll get out of this…"

Veena yawned. "But what if the aliens have the technology to hide us forever…?" she murmured. "We have to…have to…"

And then she fell asleep.

THE END

Rob led his friends to the Cryptikon entrance. "Visit Cryptikon and be terrified," said the voice of the recorded Sothoth that towered above them on the video screen.

"Been there, done that, going in for more," Rob muttered as he stepped inside.

Once through the door, the group had to ride Orbit, the fast monorail ride, to the far end of the park where the Cryptikon Zone was actually located. When they got there, Rob drew them into a huddle. "Keep your eyes peeled for real Cryptikonians," he warned them. "If they come after us, we're doomed."

"Oh really, Rob—" Veena began.

"Save it, Veena," Rob said, cutting her off. "You'll believe me soon enough." Gathering all his courage, Rob led them through the crowds, heading for the spot where he'd first seen the droopy monster. He found the fountain of black grease and passed the roses that smelled like dirty socks. *It shouldn't be far now*, he thought. *There it is!*

He'd found the path that led to the Employees Only door. Rob followed it behind the bushes, with Veena, Chanine, and Kev right behind him. But when they reached the wall beyond, there was no door. The wall was solid.

Rob stared at it in disbelief. "There was a door

• • • • • • • • •

here," he said. "It said Employees Only. I followed an alien inside…"

Veena couldn't hold it back anymore. She started to laugh. Kev joined in. "Man, Rossi, you had us going for awhile there!" Kev said. "You're quite an actor! I'm impressed!"

"But I'm not acting!" said Rob desperately.

Chanine patted his shoulder. "I believe you, Rob," she told him.

"Oh yeah, thanks," Rob said. *Chanine believes anything about anybody*, he thought miserably.

Rob Rossi spent the rest of the day at Kosmos Space Park fuming. He tried to have fun, but behind every alien face he saw only a potential threat. He knew the Cryptikonians were real. *What about the aliens in the other Zones? I'm coming back*, he decided. *I'm coming back on my own later, and I'm going to get more evidence. The whole human race might be in trouble, and somebody has to warn them…*

THE END

• • • • • • • • •

By the time they reached the office of the *Weekly World Tattler*, everybody was so tired they could hardly stand. They hobbled their way through the main reception area to the front desk. "I called just a few minutes ago," Rob told the large woman wearing a name badge that read SYLVIA. "We need to see the top editor right away."

"He's expecting you," said Sylvia. She led them down a hallway and into an office.

The editor listened with interest as Rob and the others told their story. "And here's the video I took," Rob concluded. He turned his camera around so the man could see the preview screen and hit PLAY.

The editor, whose desk plaque read TOM HONOR, nodded grimly at the four teenagers. "You've come to the right place," he told them. "This is just the kind of story we're always looking for."

Rob sighed in relief. "Good, because I think the Cryptikonians are..." His voice trailed off as he stared at Tom Honor.

Tom Honor was peeling his face off. Underneath the mask was the slimy face of a Cryptikonian. "The Cryptikonians are doing quite well, thank you," the alien hissed. "And we're always looking for stories like yours because we wouldn't want anybody to find out the truth, now would we?"

Rob and the others turned to run, only to find Sylvia the receptionist in the doorway. She had

• • • • • • • • •

taken her face mask off, too, to reveal a tangle of horrifying tentacles. "You're not going anywhere," she hissed.

"We're trapped!" Veena said as more Cryptikonians entered the room.

"Yes, you are," said the alien known as Tom Honor. "Quite probably for the rest of your lives."

THE END

• • • • • • • • •

Spun't'ii studied Chanine and Rob carefully. He walked around them, poked their legs and asked to see their hands. "Make fist," he ordered.

"Don't do it," Rob told Chanine, and he held his fingers rigid. "We have to show him he can't push us around."

Chanine would have followed Rob's example, but one of the Minutan guards aimed his ray gun. It flashed, putting a hole in the wall near Rob's head. "Okay, okay!" Chanine said, and both she and Rob made a fist.

Spun't'ii studied their arms. "You be strong," he observed. "You be useful to us."

"How?" Rob demanded, glancing nervously back at the hole in the wall.

Spun't'ii didn't answer. Instead, the Minutan guards placed devices like handcuffs on their prisoners. "Wait a minute—" Chanine began, but more little guards arrived, all with red-tipped ray guns at the ready.

"You be clever, yes," Spun't'ii told his human captives. "You be finding our secret transporter control on the Zero-G ride. Now we be needing to move it to a safer place. We not be wanting other humans to discover our plans."

"What about us?" Rob asked.

Spun't'ii activated a control that made the two wall panels close, cutting off the view of the strange

Minutan city. "We be small, so we be needing big strong workers," he said. "You be perfect for digging in the komite mines."

Rob and Chanine exchanged stunned glances.

"Komite be a delicate mineral," Spun't'ii went on. "We be not able to use machines to mine it. You be taken to the mines to join other slaves. You be spending the rest of your lives in service for the glory of the Minutan Empire."

The guards gestured for them to start walking, but Rob refused. "You can't do this!" he said. "We're not slaves! Our parents will come looking for us!"

At that, Spun't'ii laughed loud and long. "You be on planet Minuta, fool!" he cackled in amusement. "It be not mattering if *anyone* be looking for you! They *not* be finding you!"

Rob and Chanine looked at each other desperately, but there was nothing they could do. In despair, they were led away to the komite mines where they were doomed to work for the rest of their lives.

THE END

"We of Minuta be special in the Galactic Federation," he explained. "We be responsible for the great Galactic Zoo. We be collecting specimens from all planets far and wide. We be caring for them so that the peoples of the Federation be able to enjoy them."

"We have zoos, too," said Chanine. "Why don't you reveal yourselves to humans and cooperate with us? We could help you."

At that, Spun't'ii laughed. "You be not understanding. Humanity be *inferior* to us. Humanity be one of our *exhibits!*"

Rob and Chanine exchanged nervous glances. "By that you mean you're collecting specimens from our planet, right?" Rob asked the little alien. "You're looking for all kinds of animals and plants to put in all those boxes, right?"

Spun't'ii nodded. "That be correct. But we also be wanting humans for exhibit. You two be a good choice for this."

"*What?*" Chanine cried out. "You want to put us in a *cage?*"

Minutan guards stepped forward. One took Chanine's purse. Another took Rob's camera, his electronic data pad, and his cell phone. "You can't do this!" Rob told them. "We've got friends and family who will search for us! The police will come!"

Spun't'ii laughed again. "No, they be not coming for you ever." He gestured, and two human-sized

• • • • • • • • •

androids with blank faces stepped into view. "We be ready now to program these androids with your brain patterns. We also be ready to mold their faces to look like you. You be not missed." A metal cage with narrow bars was wheeled up to them, and Chanine and Rob were forced inside. "We be collecting more of you in secret," Spun't'ii added. "We be making our zoo great. Humanity be not knowing it, ever."

"Don't worry, we'll get out of this," Rob assured Chanine, but as their cage door locked with a loud click, Chanine started to cry.

"I wanted to meet real aliens," she sobbed. "Now I have, and we won't ever see home again!"

THE END

The spiral staircase was longer than it looked. By the time Veena and Kev got to the top, they were exhausted. There was a hatch in the ceiling, and they struggled to open it. But someone opened it from the other side first.

"Come on up," said a stern voice.

Veena and Kev climbed out into the last place they expected—the park security office. "You two have certainly gotten yourselves in trouble," said the uniformed woman there. Her badge read OFFICER FINN. She headed for the door. "Come with me."

Afraid to say anything, Kev and Veena followed Officer Finn out of the security building and into the park. They went all the way to the Alien Embassy to the exit turnstiles.

"You're throwing us out?" Veena asked in dismay.

"What did you expect?" Officer Finn replied.

There was another security officer waiting at the exit area, the name OFFICER WEBB on his badge. Veena and Kev gasped when they saw who was with him—Chanine and Rob.

"What did you guys do?" Chanine demanded. "We were following the…well, you know…and Officer Webb told us we had to leave the park."

"You have all broken the rules," said Officer Finn. "Visitors are not allowed beyond the normal park paths, you should know that. I'm afraid you'll never be allowed back inside Kosmos."

"But what about the underground lake?" Veena asked. "You saw us come out of there. We met real Aquarians down there!"

"You know all about them, don't you?" Kev said to the officers. "You're trying to hide it from people."

Chanine and Rob were staring at their friends in shock. "You saw *real Aquarians?*" Chanine blurted.

"Oh, please," said Officer Finn, grinning. "You don't believe that, do you? This is an amusement park, nothing more. Now please—exit the premises and do not come back." The two officers waited until all four teenagers had gone through the turnstiles. Then they began to walk away.

"*You're* Aquarians, too, aren't you?" Veena called after them. "We'll find out why you're on Earth! You can't hide forever!"

Officer Webb turned back around. "Can't we?" he said, and he saluted her. His hand was webbed.

"But…but his hand wasn't webbed a minute ago," Chanine said, watching the two officers leave.

"You were right all along, Chanine," Kev said to her. "There really are aliens on Earth, and they're right here under our noses."

Veena frowned. "Too bad nobody will believe us if we tell them."

THE END

"Are you going to arrest us?" Veena asked fearfully.

The MentalSoft employees stared at the kids. "Well, you didn't break the law," said one of the men, "but you *did* go into a clearly restricted area."

"We're sorry!" Chanine and Veena said together.

"We know that," said the woman. "So I think we'll let you go—on one condition." She paused. "Promise us that you won't tell anyone about all this."

"We promise," said Kev. "And thank you for not turning us over to security or anything."

The MentalSoft employees exchanged knowing glances. "That won't be necessary," said the man. "Just go out the door, to the left, down that corridor, and you'll see the door out. We'll stay here and take care of Gary."

Chanine sighed in relief. "Thank you. Bye, Gary! Bye, Mep Gnog!"

Kev led the way out, to the left and down the corridor. "Here's the door," he said, and opened it. "Let's not get into any more trouble, okay?"

"Hey, look," said Chanine, as she stepped outside. "My Gold Day sticker is glowing."

The others noticed that their hand stickers glowed for a moment as they passed through the door, too. Once outside on the main Transitor Zone concourse, they felt a little dizzy.

"What were we just doing?" Rob asked. "I can't remember."

"Uh…" Veena thought a moment. "We just rode Zero-G, I think."

"Yeah, that's right!" Kev said. "It was awesome! Let's go again!"

Happily, the four friends hurried back to the Zero-G ride.

THE END